I0708320

Got A Minute?

A Collection of Short Tales and Other Mind Doodles

A.P. Harper

CONTENTS

INTRODUCTION

After a year of dedicated effort, this collection has finally come together. It's a mosaic of our emotions, capturing the diverse stages we traverse in life. From moments of deep introspection and humor to frustration and righteous anger, these stories mirror the breadth of human experience. Just as life itself, they evoke laughter, sadness, and indignation. We don't confine ourselves to one genre because life isn't singular—it's a tapestry of emotions.

Each story is not just a single tale; it becomes countless narratives as it is read by many. Take what resonates with you, and leave what doesn't.

Sincerely Yours,

A.P. Harper

I

THE PUNCH

Peter Donnelly stared at the blinking cursor on the screen, waiting for him patiently to start his novel, but he had writer's block. He hadn't typed anything in weeks. His mind was numb as his doctor's gut-wrenching words echoed in his ears.

"Stage III," said the oncologist.

Peter, who was never a smoker, struggled to comprehend the diagnosis. Memories of his youth, Woodstock, and the occasional college spliff seemed a lifetime away. How could they lead to this? A nickel-sized tumor now sat on his left lung.

Dr. Harris had been blunt—perhaps too blunt. "It's difficult to treat," he admitted, though he promised to try his best. Peter longed for a glimmer of hope, something more than clinical honesty. He had so much left to do.

As an established author with more than a handful of New York Times bestsellers, Peter was at the height of his career. His biggest book deal's deadline was hanging over his head. He had six months to deliver the first draft to his agent, but he hadn't written a sentence yet. His life had split in two—before and after the diagnosis.

Peter hadn't entered the prescribed five stages of grief yet. Each morning, he waited for denial to wake up with him, but it never came. Instead, anger struck like a freight train, bypassing denial altogether. He had a title, "The Punch," but nothing more. The story of Luis Baker, a lightweight amateur boxer from the Midwest who killed a man in a barfight with a single punch, mirrored his own fight against fate. Luis became a famous boxer in prison, with televised fights and a global following.

The trouble was that Peter only had the title written, and now he was five months away from submission. He hadn't left the house for a while, and he hadn't answered his agent's calls. She was concerned about the deadline but unaware of Peter's condition and frame of mind. She wasn't the only one who didn't know. Peter hadn't told anyone—his agent, his now-adult children. No one. He didn't want to burden his loved ones, nor did he want anyone to feel sorry for him.

"Has the jury reached the verdict?" the judge asked in a monotonous tone.

The foreperson handed the paper to the clerk, who began to read, "We, the jury, find the defendant, Luis Baker, guilty of murder in the first degree."

Luis Baker's knees gave out for a second—not something he ever experienced in a ring—but today he was standing on a rug, faith yanked out from underneath his feet. Life without parole, all for one punch. But what a punch that was!

Peter reread the paragraph and shook his head. He wasn't pleased with how it read but wanted to keep the only thing he had managed to write in months. A feeling of helplessness hit, and he was ready to bargain.

Peter wasn't looking to God but to the Devil to draft up that contract. Twenty-four years in exchange for his soul, although this arrangement didn't work out for Faustus. The Devil murdered him sixteen years into the contract because Faustus wanted out. Peter wouldn't want out. He was committed, but he would take twenty—in the spirit of negotiation. He gave twenty years to Luis Baker for killing that man in the bar for poking fun at his match the night before. It seemed fair. But Peter was not Luis Baker, and not even the Devil wanted to take the deal.

Peter's acceptance of his mortality came as unexpectedly as his diagnosis after his first visit to the doctor seven months ago. The manuscript was still unfinished, despite his agent giving him a two-month extension. The drugs made him weak, nauseated, and depressed. His oncologist tried to keep him positive, as did the chemotherapy center's nurses. Peter still looked as handsome as ever but slowly faded along with his will to write. He, too, was serving life without parole, along with Luis Baker, and both would die alone in their respective prisons.

"The Punch. I like the title, Paul," said Mr. Duran from D.P. Publishing House, looking up from the pages. "Your manuscript will go to print next week. I have a good feeling about this one."

"That's promising, Frank. Just send the check to my address," said Paul Lambert, rubbing his forehead. His agent's words were encouraging.

"Sure thing. Jenny will take care of that," the publisher said, referring to the woman at the front desk.

Paul stood up and reached out for a handshake.

"When is your next book?" Mr. Duran asked.

Paul's mind drifted back to his fictional writer, Peter Donnelly, and Peter's protagonist, Luis Baker. He couldn't help but feel a pang of remorse for ending Peter's story so tragically. As he pondered his own future, he wondered if he could ever create another book as compelling or if the weight of Peter's fate would haunt his writing forever.

"I have a few errands I need to catch up on before I dive back in. Margie and I are house hunting, and I promised the boys I'd coach their junior baseball team this season," Paul said as he walked towards the door. He turned around as if he were still counting the errands on his honey-do list when a coughing fit hit him. "Oh, and I have to get this wheezing finally checked out, but I'll call you."

2

THE CASE OF THE FAIREST

Detective Valdez had a murder mystery on his hands, and it was as peculiar as they come. Snow White, the fairest of them all, had met an untimely demise, and the prime suspects? None other than the Seven Dwarves themselves. The police had called in each dwarf one by one to make a statement to shed some light on the bizarre events that had unfolded that fateful night.

Suspect No. 1: Grumpy

Grumpy scowled even more profoundly than a cat who just discovered its owner had bought a dog. He sat across from Detective Valdez, his grumpiness level surpassing even his own legendary standards.

"Alright, Grumpy," Valdez began, "you're the grumpiest of all of them. Did you hate Snow White?"

"You're a mean son of a buttery biscuit."

Valdez didn't let go. "Hated her enough to kill her?"

"If I killed her, no one would do the chores around the cottage," Grumpy retorted.

Valdez saw Grumpy's point, so he pivoted. "Alright, let's cut to the chase. What happened on the night Snow White died?"

Grumpy grunted, adjusting his hat, which seemed to have its own grumpy attitude. "We were just loungin' about, minding our own business, when she decided to have a taste of that infernal cursed apple."

Valdez leaned forward, his pen poised above his notepad like a sword, ready for battle. "A cursed apple, you say?"

Grumpy nodded, his brows furrowing so deeply they could've plowed a field. "Aye, cursed! She went all pale and collapsed faster than a soufflé during a power outage. We tried to give a hand, but what do we dwarves know about princesses and curses, besides maybe Snow White's newfound talent for taking naps?"

Valdez scribbled a note, his expression as serious as a penguin at a polar bear party. "Did you happen to spot anyone else lurking about the cottage that evening?"

Grumpy crossed his arms, clearly vexed, as if someone had stolen his favorite grump-inducing chair. "Nay, it was just us and that cursed apple. But let me tell ya, Detective, something smelled fishier than a seafood market in August, and I don't fancy fish."

Detective Valdez nodded, his curiosity as intrigued as a raccoon eyeing a trash can buffet. "A cursed apple and a suspicious aroma, you say? We'll unravel this culinary caper."

With that, Grumpy stormed out of the interrogation room, still muttering under his breath. The mystery of Snow White's demise was far from cracked, but one thing was as certain as a boiled egg—Detective Valdez had a pack of dwarves and a buffet of questions to tackle.

Suspect No. 2: Dopey

Detective Valdez didn't find anything suspicious about Grumpy's behavior other than his well-known grumpiness, but he understood that it's often the person with the bubbly personality who's featured on Dateline, and for that, he couldn't fault the dwarf. His next suspect was Dopey.

Dopey had always been the dwarf who was more interested in catching some z's than catching trouble. But today, as he lounged in the cold, metal chair of the police interrogation room, he couldn't help but feel like he'd accidentally wandered into a trippy, dopey dimension—thanks to the mushroom he ate an hour before he was called down to the station.

Detective Valdez shot him a stern look from the opposite side of the table. "Alright, Dopey, spill the beans. Did you murder Snow White?"

"Whoa dude. Slow your horses. Why would I wanna do that?"

"You tell me."

"She was the fairest of all and made some awesome brownies, dude," Dopey said, and pulled out a half-eaten fudge brownie from his pocket, crumbled to pieces, but didn't wait until Valdez could decline and stuffed it in his face.

Valdez's eyes widened like a squirrel who just discovered a tree filled with acorns on Black Friday and changed course. "I won't charge you with possession, so tell me, what went down the night Snow White died?"

Dopey blinked, his eyes resembling spinning kaleidoscopes as he tried to summon his memories—with the brownies kicking in. "Uh, like, we were all just vibing, chowing down, you know, a regular night in the chill zone. And then Snow White... she, like, munched on this apple, man. Yeah, that's the whole trip."

Valdez arched an eyebrow, his skepticism as intense as a DJ's bass drop. "Just an apple? You're totally crystal clear on that?"

Dopey scratched his head, his oversized hat drooping over his eyes like a psychedelic sunshade. "Well, it was a far-out, crimson apple. It looked totally munchable, dude."

Detective Valdez took note of the "murder weapon" that corroborated Dopey's story, but he couldn't shake the feeling that Dopey had been busier hitting the bong than concocting a devious plot. It seemed unlikely that Dopey had any motive to carry out such a serious act, and Valdez couldn't help but wonder if he was simply caught in the cosmic crossfire of a very peculiar event.

Suspect No. 3: Doc

Detective Valdez's rather trippy interview with Dopey had been quite an experience, and now he was pinning his hopes on Doc, expecting him to shed some light on what had truly happened to Snow White. After all, Doc was the brains of the operation—but did he have the means and motive to kill her?

Doc sat up straight, his round spectacles slipping down his nose as he cleared his throat. He had always been the dwarf with the big brain, the one who kept the gang from going into full-blown chaos mode. But right now, under Detective Valdez's intense scrutiny, he felt like he'd accidentally wandered into a dwarven spelling bee.

"Doc," Valdez grumbled, "you were practically rubbing shoulders with Snow White. Where were you on the night of the murder?"

"I was in the lab."

"In the lab, you say?" Detective Valdez perked up like a caffeinated kangaroo.

"I was experimenting on this mushroom Dopey picked up."

Valdez slapped his forehead in disbelief. "Alright, I'll let this drug lab slide. Did you happen to stumble upon any weirdness on that memorable night?"

Doc adjusted his glasses with the precision of a librarian handling a rare, ancient tome. "Well, Detective, the evening was shaping up to be an absolute fairytale. Snow White was... um, savoring her meal when she suddenly decided to break up with her apple."

Valdez leaned forward, his serious brows furrowing like a couple of caterpillars having a disagreement. "Broke up with her apple, you say?"

Doc cleared his throat, his voice as measured as a barista perfecting a latte. "Indeed, she began to choke on the apple as if it'd told a terrible joke. We did our darnedest to lend a hand, but, you see, we're not trained in princess-specific CPR, regrettably."

As he spoke, Doc's brain was practically doing cartwheels with thoughts, his inner scientist doing the Macarena over the riddle of Snow White's apple-related demise.

Suspect No. 4: Bashful

Bashful had always been the poster dwarf for introversion, but now, under Detective Valdez's relentless grilling, he felt like he'd won the "Most Bashful Dwarf of the Year" award.

"Bashful, we've been through this a dozen times. But one more time, for the record, where were you on the night of the murder?" Valdez asked with a stern tone.

"I was at home," said Bashful nervously.

"Alone?"

"N-No, I was with the others. Watching TV but Dopey passed out."

"What were you watching?" Valdez inquired, hoping to catch him in a lie.

"D-Dateline."

Valdez rolled his eyes like a seasoned baker kneading dough—done with the unnecessary fluff and ready to get to the heart of the matter. "How 'bout them apples? Do you know anything about it?"

"She ate it and dropped dead—that's all I know."

"Did you poison the apple?" Detective Valdez asked, looking straight at Bashful, making him more nervous than Cinderella at midnight.

Bashful fainted at the accusations, but a glass of cold water on his face woke him up. "Alright, let me ask you this. Did you spot anyone behaving all shady near the cottage that evening?"

Bashful fidgeted with his beard, his face turning a shade of red that could rival Snow White's apple. "Well, uh, I did, you know, catch a glimpse of someone... kinda', sorta'. It was this lady with a hood, and she, um, asked about Snow White. I, uh, got all flustered and just, um, pointed towards the door."

Valdez's eyes narrowed; his scrutiny unrelenting. "A lady with a hood, you say? Did you get a good look at her?"

Bashful shook his head, his voice barely louder than a mouse's whisper. "N-no, Detective, I, um, I couldn't muster the courage to meet her gaze. She, uh, made me feel all... bashful."

Detective Valdez let out a sigh and leaned back; his expression was as hopeless as the progress he was making on this case.

Suspect No. 5: Sneezy

Sneezy's nose had been throwing a full-blown fit all day, and it wasn't just because of his chronic allergies. He was on edge, and Detective Valdez's laser-focused stare was making him sneeze more than a feather pillow in a windstorm.

"Let's cut to the chase, Sneezy. Did you poison the apple?"

"With what?"

"You tell me. You're a walking biological weapon. Did you sneeze some virus on that apple?"

"How could I?" asked Sneezy. "I have to wear this mask all day."

Valdez looked at the dirty mask over Sneezy's face, which looked more like a chin holder than a shield, so he posed a different question. "Did your extraordinary sniffer pick up anything unusual that night?"

Sneezy sniffled and reached for his trusty handkerchief, which looked like it had seen more action than a circus clown's confetti cannon. "Well, Detective, I did catch a whiff of something rather peculiar. It was, um, flowery, but not the 'stop and smell the roses' type—more like someone went overboard with the perfume aisle."

Valdez leaned in, his eyes narrowing like those of a detective who'd just discovered the last piece of a jigsaw puzzle. "Perfume, you say? Can you give me the scent-sational details?"

Sneezy blew his nose with the grace of a seasoned trumpet player and took a moment to ponder. "It was, uh, flowery, I guess. Sort of like a bouquet that got into a brawl with a garden. And let me tell you, it made my usual sneezing marathon feel like a warm-up act for a fireworks display."

Suspect No. 6: Sleepy

Sleepy had always been the dwarf with a 24/7 nap schedule, but now, in the interrogation room, he was in a constant battle to keep his eyelids from staging a rebellion under Valdez's laser-focused gaze.

"Alright, Sleepy, let's wake up those memories. Where were you when Snow White met her unfortunate fate?"

"Oh, Detective, I was... um, well, I was right here, actually."

Valdez raised his eyebrows and said, "Right here? You mean at home taking a nap during a critical moment like that?"

"Well, Detective, you know how it is. I'm Sleepy for a reason," Sleepy said with a sheepish grin.

"Sleepy, do you realize the seriousness of the situation?" The detective asked and leaned closer.

Sleepy nodded, "Of course, Detective, but I couldn't help it. The comfy chair called to me, and, well, I couldn't resist."

"When you woke up, did you happen to catch any peculiar behavior from Snow White that evening?"

Sleepy yawned and stretched, as if the weight of the world rested on his shoulders. "Well, Detective, she did appear somewhat... drowsy. I mean, she'd been toiling away, and that apple... it seemed to have its own hammock or something."

Valdez sighed, clearly exasperated. "Sleepy, you're consistently in dreamland! Did you spot anyone else lurking around the cottage?"

Sleepy stifled another yawn, a heroic feat of willpower. "Sorry, Detective, I might've drifted off there. But I'm fairly certain nothing dreadful happened while I was having a nightmare about an old hag trying to sell me haunted produce."

Valdez raised an eyebrow, curiosity piqued. "A nightmare, you say? Do tell, Sleepy."

Sleepy leaned forward, his drooping eyelids showing a faint glimmer of alertness. "Well, you see, Detective, in my dream, I was at the market, and there was this ugly old woman selling fruits and veggies. But every time she handed me an apple, it cackled like a witch and tried to take a bite out of me! It was a real fruit frenzy, I tell ya."

Valdez couldn't help but crack a smile, momentarily breaking his stern demeanor. "A nightmare about a wicked produce peddler, huh? Sleepy, you're a real walking bedtime story."

Sleepy managed a drowsy grin. "Well, it's all in a day's... or rather, a night's work, Detective."

Suspect No. 7: Happy

Happy had always been the jolliest dwarf in town, but right now, he was feeling about as happy as a cat at a dog convention under Detective Valdez's interrogation spotlight.

"Happy," Valdez grumbled, "did Snow White appear distressed or fretful that night?"

Happy scratched his head, looking as befuddled as a dog trying to solve an algebra problem. "Well, Detective, she did go on about an evil queen and a poisoned apple. But I just figured she was spinning another one of her fantastical yarns, you know, like the time she swore she saw a unicorn doing karaoke."

Valdez pounded his fist on the table, making Happy's hat jump. "An evil queen and a poisoned apple? That's vital information, Happy!"

Happy shrugged, his grin refusing to take a coffee break. "Well, Detective, hindsight's a bit like trying to catch a butterfly with a fishing net. No use sobbing over spilled apple juice, right?"

As the interrogations continued, Detective Valdez realized that this case was turning into quite the fairy tale mystery. Each dwarf had their own piece of the puzzle, and it was up to him to put it all together. But one thing was for sure—this wasn't going to be your typical happily ever after, and he needed to hear what the Evil Queen had to say.

Suspect No. 8: Evil Queen

Detective Valdez sat across from the Evil Queen, a formidable character with a penchant for mirrors and, apparently, apples.

"Your Majesty," Valdez began, trying to keep a straight face, "we need to discuss Snow White's unfortunate... uh, snooze. Can you tell me what happened that evening?"

The Evil Queen's regal composure wavered for a moment, her crimson lips quivering. "Well, Detective, I might have... tried a little culinary experiment."

Valdez raised an eyebrow, suppressing a smirk. "Culinary experiment, you say? I doubt Chef Ramsey would take you into Hell's Kitchen with your poisonous ingredients. What did you intend to achieve?"

The Evil Queen let out a dramatic sigh, her flair for theatrics on full display. "Oh, Detective, I simply desired to be the fairest of them all. Snow White was... uh, competition. I wanted to level the playing field because the Grimm Brothers were useless."

Valdez couldn't help but chuckle. "Level out the playing field?"

The Evil Queen squirmed in her regal attire, beads of sweat forming on her perfectly pale brow. "Well, in hindsight, Detective, perhaps my methods were a tad... aggressive. I wanted the Prince all to myself."

Valdez leaned in, his humorless demeanor returning. "Aggressive, indeed. You'd had better luck finding love on Tinder, dear," he commented before he posed his final question. "So Your Majesty, you admit poisoning Snow White?"

The Evil Queen's shoulders slumped. "Yes, Detective, I admit it. But I never intended for her to... perish. We live in a fairy tale, after all."

With a triumphant grin, Detective Valdez leaned back. "Well, Your Majesty, it seems we've got the fairest confession of them all. You're under arrest for unlawful enchantment and accidental... sleeping, I guess."

With a resolute click of the handcuffs, justice was served, and they all lived happily ever after.

Epilogue:

As Detective Valdez wrapped up the case, he couldn't help but reflect on the peculiar nature of his profession. Here he was, solving crimes in a world where reality and fantasy blurred. It wasn't just another day at the office; it was an adventure, one that reminded him that even in the most magical of places, justice had its place.

The tale of Snow White's demise had been unraveled, but the world of fairy tales held countless more mysteries. Valdez looked up at his wall of missing persons and saw the two most recently vanished children, Hansel and Gretel. With a determined glint in his eye, he knew he was ready to dive into the next chapter.

3

DUE DATE

For Emma

I was unusually cold this January morning of 1913 in Tuskegee, Alabama. The storm that hit the northeast coast made its way south and caught everyone off guard. The two women pulled their collars higher in hopes of warmth as they stood on the side of the road. The temperature was slightly below freezing, and the streetcar was still several minutes away to pick them up for church.

"Hon', are you sure you don't want to walk? It would keep us warm," offered the older woman.

"The Lord wouldn't forgive us if we're late," said the younger one as she touched her pregnant belly through her coat. The truth was that she didn't want to walk. Her due date was near, and her feet ached. All she wanted was to sit down and rest her swollen feet. She was anxious as the date neared. She had to convince her husband not to go to Nashville for the fifty-first anniversary of the Emancipation Proclamation. It was their first child, and times were turbulent.

The Titanic sank the year before, killing approximately fifteen hundred souls on board, but this major naval disaster had a minor impact on the folks' lives in the South. They had other things occupying their minds.

Segregation was real, and it cut like a knife. Separation of races was enforced in hospitals, theaters, pools, and restaurants but extended to places no one wanted to go voluntarily—jails or mental asylums. Neighborhoods were either black or white, and so were the marriages. But nothing is ever black or white. That's a false dilemma.

"Do you remember the time when we were kids and snuck into the white church's Christmas pageant?" the older woman asked, her breath visible in the cold air.

The younger woman smiled faintly. "I do. We thought we were so clever, hiding in the back. Until Reverend Johnson found us."

"Good thing he only made us promise never to do it again," the older woman chuckled.

Segregation was life. Children were given different textbooks, adults swore on different Bibles, and jezebels of the night couldn't be color-blind regarding their clients. One couldn't even bury their dead unless it was in the designated cemetery. From dust to dust, ashes to ashes—as long as it was the right color. However, that missing footnote from the scripture was conveniently ignored.

Life was tumultuous, with the promise of progress. Democratic presidential candidate Woodrow Wilson promised fairness and justice but only delivered segregated federal offices.

Arizona became the forty-eighth state, and women could vote in all thirteen. Still, Alabama would have to wait until the 19th Amendment was ratified in 1920.

89 20
70

But life was also becoming more convenient as cars became more popular and the zipper was invented. The mayor of Tokyo gifted thousands of cherry trees to be planted in Washington, D.C., to symbolize friendship that turned sour a few years later, and black and white Oreo cookies hit the grocery stores' shelves—a risky blend of colors in a segregated life.

Times were uncertain, and the young woman was scared for her unborn child.

"You never told me what you'll name the child if it's a girl, Hon'," said the older woman as the streetcar finally approached.

The younger woman smiled and said, "Rosa. Rosa Louise Parks."

The older woman's eyes widened with approval. "That's a beautiful name. Strong and graceful."

As they boarded the streetcar, the younger woman felt a mix of anxiety and hope. The future was uncertain, but she was determined to give her child a life filled with love and opportunity, despite the harsh realities of the world they lived in.

The streetcar jolted forward, and the two women found seats together in the back reserved for the colored. The younger woman gazed out the window, her thoughts drifting to the future. "Do you think things will ever change?" she asked quietly.

The older woman placed a comforting hand on her shoulder. "Change comes slowly, but it does come. We just have to keep faith and do our part."

"Rosa will do her part," the younger woman said with a smile, her breath misting the cold window as she gazed out of the streetcar. The future may be uncertain, but with hope in her heart and determination in her soul, she believed that her daughter would help change the world.

$$4$$

THE EXHIBITION

It's the year 4023, and the myth of primitive humans inhabiting Earth until 2024 became a reality when a group of archaeologists stumbled upon a treasure trove of bizarre artifacts that left them scratching their heads, trying to make sense of their purpose. However, a group of relentless scientists has pieced together the puzzle, leading to one spectacular exhibition.

It's believed that early humans' constant egoism and negligence contributed to their ultimate demise, but further research is needed to determine the exact cause of their sudden extinction. We, the *Homo Reflectus*, embark on a journey back to an era where excess was the norm, consumerism was an extreme sport, and absurdity was practically an Olympic event. As you explore this exhibition, you'll be treated to a delightful peek into the lives of the *Homo Consumus*, those quirky folks from the 21st century.

Section 1: The Obsession with Selfies

Our journey begins with the relic known as the "selfie stick." Ah, the 21st century, a time when people would proudly extend a long pole, often adorned with the most ridiculous accessories one could imagine, to capture photos of themselves from a flattering distance. Because, you know, nothing says "I am living my best life" like a duck face taken with a neon-pink stick bedazzled with fake gemstones.

These carefully curated images, capturing the essence of spontaneity after a mere fifty tries, were then promptly shared on various social media platforms. Here, they served a crucial function: providing indisputable evidence that these individuals did, in fact, exist and occasionally left the confines of their homes. Because, let's face it, if it wasn't posted on social media, did it even happen?

Exhibit A: The Selfie Stick

Purpose: To extend one's narcissism to the world.

Function: To take pictures of oneself from unnecessarily exaggerated angles.

Social Status: Directly proportional to the length of the stick.

Obsession Level: Off the charts.

Section 2: The Dining Delirium

Ah, the 21st century, a time when food transcended its primary function of sustenance to become a tool for social validation and a testament to one's culinary prowess. Behold, the "Avocado Toast," a dish that, in its simplicity, became the crowning jewel of brunch culture. This was no ordinary toast. No, it was an art form, meticulously crafted to achieve the perfect balance of creamy avocado, a sprinkle of Himalayan pink salt, and perhaps a dash of chili flakes for the adventurous souls.

The preparation process was a ritual in itself, often accompanied by the obligatory overhead shot for Instagram, capturing the toast from its most flattering angle. For the true connoisseur, there were endless variations: topped with poached eggs, radishes sliced so thin they were practically invisible, and microgreens that added that essential touch of sophistication.

In the world of social media, this culinary masterpiece was more than just a meal; it was a statement. Posting a picture of your avocado toast wasn't just about sharing what you ate; it was about signaling to your virtual audience that you were part of an elite group who appreciated the finer things in life, like overpriced produce and artisanal bread. And let's not forget the hashtags—#Foodie, #BrunchGoals, #AvocadoMagic—each one a badge of honor in the quest for likes and validation. Because in the 21st century, your worth was often measured in double taps and heart emojis, with avocado toast being the ultimate currency.

Exhibit B: The Avocado Toast

Ingredients: Avocado, artisanal bread, a sprinkle of salt, and a drizzle of extra virgin olive oil.

Purpose: To post on Instagram.

Nutritional Value: Surprisingly high, but mainly irrelevant.

Hipster Points: Maximum if eaten in a trendy café.

Section 3: The Ubiquitous Tech Obsession

In the 21st century, *Homo Consumus* was inseparable from their gadgets. This item was found on every human remains without fail. The smartphone, a small, rectangular device that contained their entire lives, was their most cherished possession. Archaeologists of the future might be puzzled by the reverence these ancient humans had for a piece of glass and metal, but to Homo Consumus, it was nothing short of a holy relic.

Consider the smartphone, an all-powerful artifact that commands undivided attention at all times. It served as a communication hub, a navigation system, a news source, a gaming console, a personal assistant, and an endless scroll of mind-numbing content. Its power was so profound that entire social rituals were built around it. Dinners were often interrupted by the need to capture the perfect shot of a meal, and no conversation was safe from the sudden compulsion to check for the latest notification.

The smartphone had a gravitational pull that could draw its user's gaze away from anything: friends, family, and oncoming traffic. It was the first thing people reached for in the morning and the last thing they clutched before sleep, cradled lovingly like a digital teddy bear.

And let's not forget the myriad of accessories that accompanied this prized possession—cases that ranged from utilitarian to utterly ridiculous, screen protectors that promised to guard against the clumsiest of fingers, and a plethora of chargers and power banks ensuring that the device never faced the dreaded fate of a dead battery.

In the grand tapestry of 21st-century life, the smartphone was the thread that held everything together. To lose it was to face a crisis of existential proportions; to misplace it was to experience a panic akin to losing one's very identity. *Homo Consumus* might have claimed to value interpersonal relationships and nature, but in truth, their one true love was a glowing rectangle that fit snugly in their pocket.

Exhibit C: The Smartphone

Features: Social media apps, infinite cat videos, and constant notifications.

Primary Purpose: Ignoring the real world.

Secondary Purpose: Occasionally making phone calls.

Sign of Success: The number of apps installed.

Section 4: Fashion Follies

The *Homo Consumus* were renowned for their ever-evolving fashion trends, where comfort and common sense were often willingly sacrificed at the altar of "style." Exhibit D showcases 21st-century shoes, a particularly fascinating glimpse into their complex relationship with fashion.

Starting with the older female skeletal remains, we observed feet deformed by years of enduring footwear that prioritized aesthetics over anatomy. High heels, those towering symbols of elegance and suffering, were the primary culprits. Designed to elevate not just the wearer's height but also their social status, these instruments of torture squeezed toes into unnatural positions and forced arches into impossible angles. The result? Bunions, hammertoes, and a legacy of podiatric misery.

Interestingly, the obsession with painful footwear wasn't confined to women alone. In younger specimens, we discovered that male *Homo Consumus*, too, had fallen victim to the fashion craze. Although we have yet to uncover the precise motivations, we can speculate based on the evidence at hand. Perhaps it was the allure of appearing taller and more commanding, or the desire to flaunt a brand logo as a symbol of status. Or maybe, just maybe, it was the influence of social media, where influencers and celebrities paraded their latest acquisitions, making even the most impractical shoes seem like must-have items.

The footwear of the era came in all shapes and sizes, from sneakers designed with enough technology to launch a small spacecraft to absurdly impractical designer shoes that cost more than a month's rent. Sneakers, initially created for athletic purposes, had morphed into fashion statements, often limited in release and exorbitantly priced, leading to frenzied buying sprees and even altercations. These prized possessions were kept in pristine condition—some never even worn, displayed like trophies of consumerist conquest.

In the grand spectacle of 21st-century fashion, shoes were both a status symbol and a source of self-inflicted discomfort. Homo Consumus might have claimed to be walking towards the future, but it was often with a pronounced limp, thanks to their unwavering dedication to looking stylish at any cost.

Exhibit D: High Heels

Purpose: To add height and discomfort simultaneously.

Health Hazard: Frequent ankle sprains and long-term back pain.

Acceptable Occasions: Anywhere, from grocery stores to space launches.

Section 5: The Perils of Online Dating

Dating in the 21st century was an adventure in and of itself, akin to navigating a labyrinth with no map and questionable lighting. The *Homo Consumus*, ever in search of love—or at least a decent profile picture—often swiped left and right on small glowing rectangles, hoping to find their soulmate amidst a sea of selfies and filter-enhanced faces. This ritual, a cornerstone of their courtship practices, was facilitated by the primitive yet indispensable technology known as the smartphone, as showcased in Exhibit C.

Behold Exhibit E: the digital dating app, a marvel of modern matchmaking that turned the pursuit of romance into a game of visual roulette. The *Homo Consumus* would meticulously curate their online profiles, selecting photos that struck the perfect balance between candid and posed. Bios were crafted to appear witty yet sincere, peppered with hobbies that sounded more impressive than they were in reality. "Avid hiker" often translated to "went on one nature walk last year," and "foodie" was code for "takes pictures of avocado toast" (see Exhibit D for more on that phenomenon).

The process itself was both simple and complex. A swipe to the right signaled interest; a swipe to the left, rejection. The criteria for these decisions were often superficial: a charming smile, a well-groomed pet, or the elusive shirtless bathroom selfie—a genre unto itself. Matches were celebrated with a dopamine rush, a fleeting victory in the relentless quest for connection.

However, the journey didn't end there. Once a match was made, the real adventure began. Conversations initiated with the evergreen opener, "Hey," would teeter on the brink of awkwardness, each party trying to gauge the other's level of interest and sanity. Creative attempts to stand out might include sending memes or discussing the merits of pineapple on pizza, a topic as divisive as any political debate.

And then there were the dates themselves, meticulously planned to appear spontaneous. The *Homo Consumus* would meet in dimly lit bars or bustling cafes, their heads buried in their smartphones as they waited for their potential partner to arrive. First impressions were critical, yet often overshadowed by the constant need to document the experience on social media. If a tree falls in a forest and no one is around to hear it, does it make a sound? Similarly, if a date goes well but isn't posted on Instagram, did it really happen?

In the grand tapestry of 21st-century life, dating apps were a thread woven with hope, humor, and a touch of desperation. The *Homo Consumus* might have been on a quest for love, but more often than not, they found themselves entangled in a web of awkward encounters and ghosting. Yet, ever the optimists, they continued to swipe, ever hopeful that their next right swipe might just lead to happily ever after—or at least a good story for their next brunch.

Exhibit E: The Dating Profile

Key Elements: Heavily filtered photos, exaggerated hobbies, and witty one-liners.

Purpose: To find love, or failing that, to finally discover if your pet iguana's opinion on world politics is truly as riveting as you claim in your profile.

Reality vs. Expectation: Often a surprise.

Success Rate: Highly variable.

Section 6: Environmental Irony

Despite the mounting evidence of climate change and environmental degradation, the *Homo Consumus* continued to engage in activities that seemingly hastened their own demise. Among their most baffling customs was a peculiar reverence for plastic. It's as if they believed the gods and goddesses of the land and sea required offerings of plastic, which they dutifully provided in unmeasurable quantities. This Exhibit F, showcasing a plethora of discarded plastic artifacts, suggests that these ancient humans engaged in a ritualistic dumping of plastic waste, a practice that transcended generations.

Archaeological digs reveal oceans and rivers teeming with plastic debris, leading us to hypothesize that *Homo Consumus* enjoyed swimming amidst these colorful remnants. Perhaps it was their version of an underwater treasure hunt, where the objective was to find the most unusual piece of plastic flotsam. The sheer variety—bottles, bags, straws, and countless other items—points to a society that embraced plastic with fervent dedication, possibly viewing it as a status symbol or a badge of modernity.

Our studies indicate that plastic not only held religious significance but also played a role in leisurely activities, although we have yet to decipher the exact rules of this mysterious game. Did they compete to see who could collect the most plastic in a single dive? Or perhaps they fashioned makeshift sculptures, turning their waste into ephemeral art pieces displayed briefly before returning to the waves?

Beyond the aquatic realm, *Homo Consumus* displayed a fondness for plastic in their everyday lives. Their homes were filled with single-use items, from utensils to packaging, suggesting a culture of convenience that overshadowed environmental concerns. They even went as far as wrapping individual fruits in plastic, a practice that surely amused the gods of irony.

Despite the clear and present danger posed by their plastic addiction, *Homo Consumus* persisted, perhaps believing that their plastic offerings would appease the deities and stave off ecological collapse. Or maybe they were simply too enamored with the convenience and versatility of plastic to consider the long-term consequences.

In the grand scheme of 21st-century life, the reverence for plastic is one of the most curious aspects of *Homo Consumus*. While their civilization ultimately faced significant challenges due to their environmental practices, we can only marvel at their unwavering commitment to plastic—a material that, much like their legacy, has endured through the ages. And so, we continue to study these relics, piecing together the story of a society that thrived on convenience and left behind a lasting, albeit perplexing, legacy of plastic.

Exhibit F: The Disposable Water Bottle

Purpose: To provide a fleeting moment of hydration.

Environmental Impact: Incalculable.

Alternative: Reusable bottles were readily available but rarely used.

Section 7: The Entertainment Epidemic

The 21st century was marked by an insatiable appetite for entertainment, a time when *Homo Consumus* dedicated their lives to the pursuit of endless amusement. Our findings suggest that these ancient humans spent countless hours binge-watching television series and scrolling through an infinite cascade of cat memes. Evidence of this behavior is strikingly evident in Exhibit G: the ubiquitous couch.

These artifacts were discovered in every living quarter, each one boasting a curious feature—bottom-shaped bumps in the seating area. We believe this was not a result of the original design but rather the imprint of many a marathon viewing session. Imagine, if you will, the daily ritual: *Homo Consumus* returning from their various daily toils, only to collapse into the welcoming embrace of their well-worn sofas.

The binge-watching phenomenon was fueled by an impressive arsenal of streaming services, offering a veritable smorgasbord of visual content. Entire weekends could vanish in the blink of an eye as these humans devoured season after season of their favorite shows. Cliffhangers were no match for the "Next Episode" button, a siren call that lured them deeper into the abyss of serial story-telling.

But it wasn't just dramatic sagas and sitcoms that held their attention. No, the *Homo Consumus* had a particular fondness for videos of cats. Cats, doing all manner of things—playing piano, knocking over vases, wearing tiny hats. These feline antics provided endless amusement, proving that no matter how advanced their technology became, a cat falling off a table remained the pinnacle of comedy.

Of course, their entertainment diet wasn't without its side effects. The aforementioned bottom-shaped bumps were just the beginning. There was also the phenomenon known as "binge fatigue," a condition characterized by glazed eyes, numb posteriors, and an overwhelming sense of having accomplished absolutely nothing. Yet, despite these drawbacks, the allure of just one more episode was irresistible.

Further examination of Exhibit G reveals other clues to their entertainment habits. Crumbs nestled in the crevices hint at a companion activity—snacking. Bags of chips, bowls of popcorn, and an array of sugary delights were essential components of the *Homo Consumus* entertainment experience. The more elaborate setups even included built-in cup holders and strategically placed blankets, ensuring that comfort was never compromised during these extended viewing sessions.

In the grand narrative of 21st-century life, the pursuit of entertainment stands out as a defining characteristic. *Homo Consumus* may have faced numerous challenges, but they met them with a remote in one hand and a snack in the other. And while they may not have moved much from their well-worn couches, their imaginations traveled far and wide, exploring the countless worlds brought to life on their screens. So, as we study these artifacts, we gain insight into a society that valued relaxation, escapism, and, above all, the simple joy of a good cat meme.

Exhibit G: The Couch Potato's Throne

Features: Plush cushions, built-in cup holders, and remote-control pockets.

Purpose: To encourage sloth-like behavior.

Consequences: Reduced muscle mass and a distorted sense of time.

Section 8: The Illusion of Productivity

Based on the evidence we've uncovered, it's clear that *Homo Consumus* were masters of the art of boasting about productivity while expertly procrastinating on various digital platforms. These ancient humans created elaborate spaces they called "offices," which, judging by the wear and tear on their ergonomic chairs and the accumulation of coffee mugs, they spent more time in than their actual living quarters. However, our findings indicate that very little was actually achieved within these walls.

Exhibit H presents a typical office setup, complete with dual monitors, an array of colorful sticky notes, and an assortment of stress-relief gadgets that hint at their constant state of distraction. These "offices" were equipped with everything needed to give the illusion of hard work, yet closer inspection reveals the true nature of their activities.

The evidence shows that a significant portion of their time was spent toggling between social media sites, online shopping, and watching videos of unlikely animal friendships. The browser history from these ancient computers paints a vivid picture: hours dedicated to deep dives into obscure Wikipedia articles, followed by frantic last-minute attempts to meet deadlines. The term "productivity theater" seems apt, as these spaces were more about the performance of being busy than actually getting things done.

Further analysis of their digital correspondence reveals an interesting pattern. The *Homo Consumus* would frequently send emails filled with jargon and buzzwords, carefully crafted to sound impressive while saying very little. Meetings were another favorite pastime, often scheduled back-to-back, creating the perfect cover for avoiding real work. These gatherings were usually long on discussion and short on decision-making, a testament to their collective knack for turning simple tasks into Herculean endeavors.

Even their office attire was part of the charade. Business casual, as they called it, was a delicate balance between looking professional and being comfortable enough to take a midday nap. The "work-from-home" era added another layer to this dynamic, with video calls conducted in professional-looking shirts paired with pajama bottoms—hidden from view, of course.

And let's not forget the office culture. Breaks were an integral part of the workday, often stretching well beyond their intended length. The infamous "water cooler talk" became a ritual, where gossip and small talk flourished. It was here that they perfected the art of appearing busy while actually doing very little—an achievement in its own right.

In conclusion, while the *Homo Consumus* may have prided themselves on their industriousness, the reality was a bit more relaxed. Their "offices" were less about output and more about maintaining the illusion of productivity. As we study these relics, we can only marvel at their sophisticated balance of work and procrastination, a delicate dance that defined their unique approach to modern life.

Exhibit H: The Open Office Plan

Purpose: To foster collaboration and destroy concentration.

Actual Outcome: A cacophony of noise and a rise in workplace stress.

Redemption: Noise-canceling headphones.

Section 9: The Rise of the Delivery Culture

In the 21st century, *Homo Consumus* could summon almost anything with the touch of a button. The concept of "home delivery" reached such absurd heights that it bordered on magical realism. Our excavations reveal that they could order virtually anything their imaginations conjured up. Food, medicine, activity boxes, and even a spouse—all could be delivered directly to their doorstep with astonishing speed and efficiency.

Exhibit I showcases a collection of delivery devices, ranging from drones to robotic couriers, each designed to cater to the insatiable demand for instant gratification. *Homo Consumus* developed an extraordinary reliance on these services, a testament to their preference for convenience over effort. No longer did they need to venture out into the world to satisfy their desires; instead, they could remain comfortably ensconced in their homes while everything they wanted came to them.

The variety of items available for delivery was staggering. Craving sushi at 3 AM? No problem. Need a new set of bed linens because you spilled that sushi? Easily fixed. Their penchant for ordering food was legendary, leading to an entire industry of delivery apps that catered to every culinary whim. And it wasn't just food. If they needed medicine, they could summon it with the same ease, ensuring that even the slightest hint of a headache wouldn't require them to leave their couch. Refer back to Exhibit G, the Couch Potato's Throne.

But the offerings didn't stop at essentials. The *Homo Consumus* had a flair for the extravagant and the unnecessary. Monthly subscription boxes provided a constant stream of curated surprises, from gourmet snacks to obscure hobbies. Want to learn how to knit or brew your own beer? There was a box for that, delivered with all the supplies and instructions you'd need—assuming you ever got around to opening it.

And then there were the more peculiar deliveries. Our records indicate that in some regions, it was possible to order a spouse. Yes, you read that correctly. Online services promised to deliver the perfect partner, tailored to one's specifications. Whether it was a marketing gimmick or a genuine attempt at matchmaking, it reflects the extent to which *Homo Consumus* embraced the convenience of delivery culture.

The delivery frenzy didn't stop with just goods and services. Entire lifestyles were built around the convenience of home delivery. Fitness enthusiasts could have gym equipment and personal trainers brought to their doorstep. Aspiring chefs could receive fresh ingredients and recipes, turning their kitchens into gourmet restaurants. Even entertainment was delivered—streaming services ensured a constant flow of movies and series, eliminating the need to ever leave home for a theater.

In conclusion, *Homo Consumus'* mastery of home delivery is a fascinating study in convenience culture. They transformed their homes into hubs of instant satisfaction, where the push of a button could fulfill their every whim. As we delve deeper into their history, we can only marvel at their ingenuity and the sheer audacity of their delivery-dependent lifestyle.

Exhibit I: The Food Delivery App

Delivery Time: Faster than cooking but slower than microwave popcorn.

Purpose: To satisfy cravings for gourmet cuisine, greasy indulgences, or a bizarre fusion of both, all without leaving your couch.

Occasions: Anytime, anywhere, even during weddings and funerals.

Impact on Waistlines: Significant.

Section 10: The Fitness Fad

Despite their predominantly sedentary lifestyles, the *Homo Consumus* had a peculiar obsession with fitness trends, ranging from the intense rigors of CrossFit to the steamy confines of hot yoga studios. They created an entire "fitness industry" dedicated to the pursuit of physical perfection. Ironically, while their waistlines continued to expand, their fixation on fitness showed no signs of shrinking.

Our most exciting discovery thus far is Exhibit J, a collection of gym equipment. These became icons of the era, embodying the blend of earnestness and absurdity that characterized their approach to fitness.

The *Homo Consumus* frequented gyms outfitted with every conceivable piece of equipment, yet many found solace in the promise of shortcut devices like the Shake Weight. It was marketed with fervent zeal, promising results with minimal effort—a dream come true for a society that valued convenience above all. Infomercials featured impeccably toned individuals demonstrating its use, shaking their way to sculpted arms in slow motion. The sight was both hypnotic and hilarious, a testament to the lengths *Homo Consumus* would go to avoid traditional exercise.

Beyond Shake Weight, the fitness industry was a smorgasbord of fads and trends. CrossFit enthusiasts could be found flipping tires and lifting weights in warehouses-turned-gyms, their dedication evident in the constant stream of selfies showcasing their sweaty exertions. Hot yoga practitioners contorted themselves in sweltering studios, emerging red-faced and drenched yet spiritually uplifted by the experience.

Then there were the fitness influencers, a peculiar breed of *Homo Consumus* who built empires on social media platforms. They offered daily doses of inspiration, workout routines, and dietary advice, all wrapped up in perfectly filtered photos and motivational quotes. Their followers, desperate for a piece of the fitness pie, would dutifully like, share, and attempt to emulate their regimes, often with mixed results.

Fitness classes became social events, with *Homo Consumus* flocking to trendy spin classes, Zumba sessions, and boot camps. These gatherings were as much about community and competition as they were about exercise. Wearing the latest activewear and armed with the newest gadgets, they transformed workouts into performances, each bead of sweat a badge of honor.

However, the reality behind this fitness frenzy was often less glamorous. Despite the hours spent in gyms and studios, many *Homo Consumus* struggled with their weight and overall health. The convenience of fast food and the lure of binge-watching marathons often counteracted their best efforts. Yet, their dedication to the pursuit of fitness remained unwavering, a curious contradiction in their lifestyle.

In the grand narrative of *Homo Consumus*, the fitness obsession stands as a testament to their desire for self-improvement and their susceptibility to clever marketing. The Shake Weight, symbolizes this era perfectly—a blend of hope, humor, and the perpetual quest for an easy fix. As we study these artifacts, we gain insight into a society that, despite its flaws, never stopped striving for betterment, even if it often took the path of least resistance.

Exhibit J: Gym equipment

Purpose: To provide a comical workout and occasional laughter.

Effectiveness: Debated but highly entertaining.

Collectible Value: Rare and sought after by future archaeologists.

Section 11: Food That Defied Time

Our final section presents a truly mind-boggling phenomenon of the 21st century—the fast food that never spoiled! While the *Homo Consumus* were busy snapping selfies, procrastinating in their pseudo-offices, and shaking their way to fitness with contraptions like the Shake Weight, they also managed to create food that could withstand the test of time. Exhibit K showcases these indestructible culinary marvels, perfectly preserved as if they were freshly made yesterday. But don't let appearances deceive you. While these fast-food relics look as fresh as the day they were created, *Homo Consumus* missed the mark when it came to taste and nutrition.

Our researchers were initially baffled by the immaculate condition of these items. Burgers with lettuce still crisp, fries that retained their golden hue, and buns without a hint of mold—all seemed immune to the natural process of decay. It was only upon closer examination that we uncovered the truth: these foods were more chemically engineered than naturally cooked.

Take the ubiquitous burger, for instance. Its enduring freshness can be attributed to a cocktail of preservatives and additives designed to extend shelf life indefinitely. While *Homo Consumus* enjoyed the convenience of fast food, the nutritional value left much to be desired. A diet rich in such fare often led to expanding waistlines, contradicting their parallel obsession with fitness.

The resilience of these fast-food items sparked numerous urban legends. Some *Homo Consumus* believed that a single fast-food meal, buried in a time capsule, would serve as a perfect meal for future generations. Others joked that, in the event of an apocalypse, fast food would outlast humanity itself, providing sustenance for whatever species might come next.

Our examination of these fast-food artifacts also uncovered the cultural rituals surrounding their consumption. Drive-thrus became modern-day watering holes where *Homo Consumus* would gather, often in their vehicles, to partake in these quick, satisfying, yet nutritionally dubious meals. The phenomenon of "supersizing" portions reflected their desire for more—more convenience, more flavor, and more calories—all in a single sitting.

Marketing campaigns played a significant role in the fast-food frenzy. Brightly colored advertisements featuring smiling families and catchy jingles created an illusion of wholesome, happy meals. The reality, however, was a stark contrast. Despite the convenience, regular consumption of fast food was linked to a host of health issues, from obesity to heart disease. Yet, the allure of a meal ready in minutes, without the hassle of cooking or cleaning, was simply too strong to resist.

The persistence of fast food in *Homo Consumus'* diet also highlights their complex relationship with time and effort. In a world where instant gratification was the norm, the slow, deliberate process of preparing a meal was often seen as an unnecessary burden. Fast food provided a quick fix, a way to keep pace with their hectic lives filled with social media scrolling, pseudo-productivity, and fitness fads.

In conclusion, the fast food phenomenon of the 21st century offers a fascinating glimpse into the paradoxes of *Homo Consumus.* They were a society that valued convenience over quality, appearance over substance, and speed over sustainability. As we study these indestructible food relics, we are reminded of the delicate balance they struck between innovation and excess, a legacy preserved in every unspoiled fry and eternally fresh burger.

Exhibit K: Cheeseburger with Fries, Extra Large

Contents: Perfectly intact hamburgers with what we believe is cheese, and fries.

Purpose: To serve as a time capsule of questionable culinary choices, preserving the essence of gluttony for generations to come.

Preservation Secret: A carefully engineered blend of preservatives, chemicals, and culinary wizardry designed to outlast our wildest nightmares.

Lifespan: Eons, apparently.

Taste: Well, let us just say it is a taste that refuses to be forgotten.

Epilogue

As you conclude your journey through this Exhibition, you may find yourself marveling at how an entire civilization could be

so simultaneously ingenious and absurd. The 21st-century *Homo Consumus*, with their peculiar habits and bizarre obsessions, offer a rich tapestry of contradictions that leave us with a profound lesson about the consequences of unchecked consumerism and the vital importance of reflecting on our own choices and embracing conservation.

These ancient humans managed to create groundbreaking technologies, from smartphones that could summon anything from sushi to spouses, to fitness gadgets that promised rock-hard abs with minimal effort. Yet, their brilliance was often overshadowed by their baffling priorities. They spent hours binge-watching TV shows and scrolling through an endless stream of cat memes, all while boasting about their productivity in pseudo-offices designed more for procrastination than performance.

Their relationship with food was equally perplexing. The *Homo Consumus* excelled in the creation of fast food that never spoiled, a testament to their ability to engineer meals that could withstand the apocalypse. Burgers and fries preserved in pristine condition are relics of a culture that valued convenience over nutrition, and appearance over substance. It's as if they believed that if it looked good and arrived quickly, the actual content didn't matter.

Fitness was another arena where their contradictions shone brightly. Despite leading sedentary lives filled with ergonomic chairs and streaming marathons, they harbored an obsession with fitness trends. From CrossFit to hot yoga, they pursued the latest fads with fervent dedication, all while their waistlines continued to expand. Devices like the Shake Weight promised effortless transformation, embodying the *Homo Consumus'* eternal quest for shortcuts.

Perhaps the most telling aspect of their culture was their reverence for plastic. They seemed to worship this versatile material, offering it to the gods of land and sea by dumping it in unmeasurable quantities. Plastic was everywhere—in their homes, their oceans, and even their food. The environmental consequences of their actions were dire, yet they persisted, driven by an insatiable appetite for convenience and disposability.

As we reflect on the *Homo Consumus*, we are reminded of the delicate balance between innovation and sustainability. Their legacy is a cautionary tale about the dangers of unchecked consumerism and environmental neglect. Their ingenious yet absurd practices serve as a mirror, prompting us to examine our own habits and make more conscious choices.

So, as you leave this Exhibition, take with you not just the humor and sarcasm with which we have explored this bygone era, but also a sense of urgency to learn from their mistakes. Let the story of the 21st-century *Homo Consumus* inspire you to embrace conservation, prioritize sustainability, and strive for a future where brilliance isn't overshadowed by absurdity. If there is one thing we can glean from their legacy, it's the importance of finding harmony between progress and preservation, ensuring that our own civilization doesn't become a cautionary tale for future generations.

5

THE BLACKOUT

"I am speaking to you from the Cabinet Room of 10 Downing Street. This morning, the British Ambassador in Berlin handed the German Government a final note, stating that unless we heard back from them by 11 o'clock that they were prepared at once to withdraw their troops from Poland, a state of war would exist between us. I have to tell you now that no such undertaking has been received and that, consequently, this country is at war with Germany." Neville Chamberlain's voice crackled through the radio on September 3rd, 1939, as the entire country huddled over the speakers, listening with horror as the Prime Minister announced that Britain was at war with Germany. The twenty-five-year-old Royal Air Force volunteer, Gordon Frederick Cummins, along with his fellow airmen, looked at each other, pondering what this would mean for them in the years to come.

As the clouds of war darkened the horizon, Gordon's emotions churned like the tempestuous English Channel. He had joined the RAF with dreams of heroism and a profound sense of duty, but now, with the world at war, the reality of conflict weighed heavily on his conscience. The camaraderie with his fellow servicemen brought some solace, but the fear of the unknown gnawed at him. Gordon earned the nickname 'The Duke' because of his boastful attitude and false claims of nobility, which made him quite unpopular among his peers. All he wanted to do was live the life of an aristocrat, and the war did not help him achieve his dreams. In 1941, while stationed in Colerne, Wiltshire, he often visited pubs in London's West End, where he sought the comfort of the ladies of the night. Here, he met a nineteen-year-old clerk named Maple Churchyard, who made an extra living working as a prostitute at night. Gordon became a frequent visitor to Maple.

The German air raids over London brought with them an era of darkness, both literal and figurative. The city was plunged into a blackout, with all lights extinguished to prevent enemy aircraft from finding their targets. The blackout curtains, the dimmed streetlights, and the eerie silence of a city hiding from the sky created an atmosphere of dread. It was during these blackouts that the true nature of Gordon's darkness revealed itself. The murder cases began to surface amidst the bombings' chaos. Women, many of them working in the shadows of the night, began to disappear. Their bodies were found in alleys, parks, and abandoned buildings, each bearing the marks of a meticulous yet ruthless killer. The London Metropolitan Police were already stretched thin by the war effort, but the rising body count demanded their immediate attention.

Detective Inspector Arthur Vickery, a seasoned investigator with a sharp mind and an unyielding sense of justice, was assigned to lead the investigation. Alongside him was Detective Sergeant William Harris, a younger but equally determined officer known for his attention to detail and persistence. Vickery and Harris had seen their share of gruesome cases, but the wartime murders carried a chilling brutality that set them apart. They poured over each crime scene, sifting through the scant evidence available. The blackouts made their work infinitely harder, obscuring potential witnesses and crucial details. Every lead seemed to end in darkness, much like the city they patrolled. Yet they pressed on, knowing that each night the killer remained free, another life was at risk.

For Gordon, the blackouts were a twisted blessing. The darkness provided the perfect cover for his malevolent urges. He moved through the shadowy streets with a predatory grace, his RAF uniform granting him a veneer of respectability that deflected suspicion. The thrill of the hunt consumed him, and the war-torn city became his hunting ground. Despite the chaos of the bombings, Gordon's meticulous nature allowed him to leave behind little evidence. He reveled in the fear that gripped the city, knowing that he was the unseen specter haunting the streets. His interactions with Maple became more frequent, her vulnerability heightening his sense of power.

As the investigation deepened, Gordon's name surfaced. His false aristocratic airs, his frequent visits to the West End, and his dubious alibis drew the detectives' attention. Vickery and Harris began to piece together a profile of their suspect, a man who hid his monstrous nature behind a facade of charm and respectability. The detectives' pursuit of Gordon intensified, with each clue bringing them closer to the truth. They delved into his past, uncovering a history of deceit and manipulation. Interviews with his fellow airmen revealed a man with conceits of grandeur and a simmering resentment towards those who rejected him. Gordon, sensing the tightening noose, grew bolder in his attacks.

The thrill of evading capture fueled his actions, but so did a growing paranoia. He watched the detectives from the shadows, studying their movements, anticipating their next steps. The blackouts, once his ally, now seemed to close in on him, turning the darkness into a prison rather than a sanctuary.

As London endured the relentless bombings, the city held its breath, waiting for the moment when the darkness would lift and the killer would be brought to justice. Detective Inspector Vickery and Detective Sergeant Harris knew that time was running out. The final confrontation between the hunters and the hunted loomed, promising a reckoning that would echo through the war-ravaged streets of London.

One rainy night in October 1941, as Gordon and Maple sat in a dimly lit pub, the tension in the air was palpable. The news from the front lines was grim, and the blitz had left its mark on the city and its people. Maple's usual cheerfulness seemed subdued as she sipped her drink, her eyes distant. Gordon's mind, however, was elsewhere. He was unaware that his days of terrorizing the city were numbered. The detectives were closing in on him, but Maple was too smitten to see the obvious signs of Gordon's psyche.

The breakthrough came when a witness—a young boy who had been hiding in a nearby alley during one of Gordon's attacks—came forward. The boy had seen a man in an RAF uniform leave the scene, his face partially illuminated by a flickering streetlamp. It was a small but crucial piece of evidence. Armed with this new information, Vickery and Harris focused their investigation on RAF personnel stationed in and around London. They conducted interviews and background checks, scrutinizing every detail. Gordon's unusual behavior and frequent visits to the

West End sparked suspicion. They were able to obtain a warrant to search his quarters.

Inside Gordon's quarters, the detectives found damning evidence. Hidden in a locked drawer were items belonging to the victims—trinkets, pieces of clothing, and photographs. Each item told the story of a life brutally cut short. The detectives' hearts hardened with resolve as they realized the extent of Gordon's depravity. They also found a notebook meticulously detailing his crimes. The chilling entries described each murder with clinical precision, revealing Gordon's twisted satisfaction. The evidence was overwhelming. Vickery and Harris knew they'd found their man.

Gordon was arrested at his airbase; his once-confident demeanor shattered as he was led away in handcuffs. The news of his capture spread quickly, bringing a sense of relief to the city. The serial killer, who had exploited the cover of darkness, was finally brought to light. Gordon Frederick Cummins' trial was a sensation. The courtroom was packed with journalists, curious onlookers, and the families of the victims. Gordon, ever the performer, maintained an air of arrogance, but his bravado crumbled as the evidence was presented.

Detective Inspector Vickery and Detective Sergeant Harris testified, detailing the painstaking investigation that led to Gordon's capture. The witness testimony, the physical evidence, and Gordon's own notebook painted a damning picture. The jury deliberated for only a few hours before returning a guilty verdict. Gordon Frederick Cummins was sentenced to death. In June 1942, he was hanged at Wandsworth Prison. His execution brought a sense of closure to the victims' families and the city of London, which had endured so much during the war.

Detective Inspector Arthur Vickery and Detective Sergeant William Harris continued their work, their partnership strengthened by the ordeal they had faced. The war raged on, but the streets of London were a little safer without the shadow of the Blackout Killer. Gordon's story became a cautionary tale, a reminder of the darkness that can lurk within even the most seemingly respectable individuals. The detectives knew their work was far from over, but they found solace in knowing that light had triumphed over darkness and that one day, London's nights would shine bright again.

6

A WEEK IN HAIKU

Sunday's here at last
A day of rest, chill, and peace,
Socks on, day off, yeah.

Monday morning blues,
Meetings, work, coffee's my muse,
Eight hours to amuse.

Tuesday, midweek hump,
Longing for the weekend's jump,
Endless tasks to plump.

Wednesday, oh halfway,
The weekend's not far away,
Survive one more day.

Thursday creeps along,
Almost there, can't go wrong,
Weekend's siren song.

Friday, time to play,
Freedom's just hours away,
Weekend's here to stay.

Saturday, no strife,
Fun and joy throughout my life,
Best day, love my wife.

7

THE WIDOW

"**M**rs. Stafford... Ma'am, I'm sorry for your loss, but I have to ask a few questions surrounding your husband's death." Det. Turner tried to console the hysterical woman.

Mrs. Lynn Stafford was in shock after her husband of twelve years, Jason Stafford, a Special Forces Medical Sergeant, an 18-Delta, was mauled to death by his beloved two Dalmatians.

'Jace the Blade,' as everyone called him, was in his mid-thirties and looked forward to returning from his final tour in Afghanistan. As a Green Beret, not only was Jace an elite sniper but also the best trauma specialist in all five Special Forces groups. He was the finest first responder in the world. Jace got his moniker while in training because a fellow student's appendix was within minutes of rupturing during the isolation phase of their training. Within a blink of an eye, Jason cut the student open and performed an emergency appendectomy right there and then. The 5th Special Forces Group in Fort Campbell, Kentucky, was lucky to have him. He completed so many tours in Afghanistan that he lost count. His retirement neared, but that left him with mixed feelings. His marriage was on the rocks, and he felt more comfortable on the battlefield than in his living room. He needed war like a fish needs water.

He did not miss his wife, Lynn, but sure longed for his two adorable, movie-perfect Dalmatians, Mike and Ike. Jace found it hilarious that he named the puppies after a well-known fruit-flavored candy brand, Mike and Ike.

"Mrs. Stafford," said the detective to the woman, who was now in a calmer state of mind, "I know it's difficult, but I need you to describe exactly what happened."

"Jason has been home for about a month but has had difficulty adjusting to home life. He probably had PTSD, but he was too vain and proud to admit it," Lynn lied about his emotional state. Jace was fine. Mrs. Stafford explained to the detective that it started like any other weekday. When she returned home around 4 p.m. after getting up and leaving for work around 7 a.m., she discovered Jason lying in a pool of blood in the living room with the dogs lying next to him, both of whom had blood stains on their black-dotted fur. The woman wailed out at the memory.

Witnesses at Lynn's work and the coroner corroborated her story, and her husband's death was ruled an accident. Mrs. Stafford received a hefty sum from Jason's life insurance policies and will receive a lifetime annuity through the Survivor Benefit Program. By the time everything settled, Mrs. Stafford had become the owner of two million dollars.

Mike and Ike were immediately euthanized, although the detective's dog-loving heart had difficulty accepting that it had to be done. Dalmatians? Really? Not Pitbulls, Rottweilers, or German Shepherds, but Dalmatians? He saw the two dogs sitting calmly and obediently next to Mrs. Stafford as he walked out of the house, not indicating any aggression towards her or any of the strangers that came in and out of the house all through the evening, and that strange feeling stayed with him.

As Detective Turner drove away, he couldn't shake the feeling that something was off. "Dalmatians mauling their owner? It doesn't add up," he muttered to himself. His gut told him to dig deeper, but the case was closed, and his hands were tied.

Mrs. Stafford closed the door of a small U-Haul truck and looked back at the house she had just sold. She was on her way to her dream beach house in South Carolina as a widow, with her lover of several years waiting for her on the other end. Finally, they could be together. Jason would have never agreed to the divorce despite no longer loving her, and without children, Lynn felt trapped in a marriage that did not exist. She wanted a family. Jason did not. All he cared about was those damn dogs. She hated them.

During Jace the Blade's last assignment, Lynn slowly and deliberately trained both dogs to fear Jason and protect her at all costs.

Tires in the back were used to make Mike and Ike stronger, and a lifelike ragdoll of Jace hung from them. Lynn and her boyfriend used Jason's favorite song to create the attack and kill reflex in the dogs. After he returned, it was only a matter of time before Jason played his favorite tunes, and on that fateful morning, he did. The months-long training activated in that instant, and the dogs launched at his throat, and Jason bled out in the living room. "Terrible accident," everyone said, and paid their condolences to the grieving widow.

As Lynn drove towards her new life, she glanced at the empty passenger seat and allowed herself a small, satisfied smile. She had played her part well, fooling everyone around her. Her thoughts drifted to her lover waiting for her, and she felt a surge of excitement. Her plan had worked perfectly. She was free.

Back in his office, Detective Turner stared at the case file on his desk. Something about it still didn't sit right with him. He picked up his phone and dialed a number. "Hey, it's Turner. I need a favor. Can you pull all the records on the Stafford case? Yeah, I know it's closed, but I've got a feeling."

8

GENERATIONOLOGY

Welcome to the world of generationology, where each generation weaves its own vibrant thread into the fabric of history. In this tale, we will explore the unique characteristics of the G.I. Generation, Silent Generation, Baby Boomers, Generation X, Millennials, Generation Z, and the emerging Generation Alpha. We'll delve into their diverse tastes, customs, manners, music, technology, and humor, celebrating the differences and finding the common threads that connect us all. Through their stories, we'll reveal the rich and ever-evolving mosaic of human connection and historical heritage that defines us.

G.I. Generation (Born 1900–1924)

Taste: The G.I. Generation's taste is an ode to simplicity and timeless elegance, reminiscent of the charm found in black-and-white movie marathons. Their culinary preferences lean towards the hearty and familiar, with classic dishes like meatloaf and mashed potatoes being staples that evoke comfort and nostalgia. Their coffee habits are equally robust, preferring brews that could jolt even a hibernating bear awake, showcasing their love for strong, no-nonsense flavors.

Customs: Renowned for their impeccable manners, they possess a level of courtesy that could put a professional butler to shame. Their sense of duty and discipline was forged during the trials of World War II, instilling in them a profound respect for order and responsibility. This generation is often seen as the original "savers," a trait that sometimes borders on hoarding. They stockpile everyday items like rubber bands and buttons with the same seriousness as doomsday preppers, always prepared for an uncertain future.

Manners: Politeness is the hallmark of this generation, almost to the point of being a superpower. They hold traditional etiquette in the highest regard, to the extent that they would prefer to scale a mountain made of barbed wire than to interrupt a conversation or leave the house in anything less than a perfectly pressed suit. Their commitment to civility and proper conduct is unwavering, reflecting a bygone era of refinement and respect.

Music: Swing music holds a special place in their hearts. The big band sounds and smooth crooning of artists like Frank Sinatra served as the soundtrack to their formative years. Even today, they can light up a dance floor with the energy and precision of twirling tornadoes, their feet moving instinctively to the rhythms that defined their youth. For them, these melodies are not just music but a cherished connection to the past.

Technology: The G.I. Generation has witnessed an incredible evolution in technology, from a time when "streaming" referred to a flowing brook to the advent of the internet and smartphones. They have approached these advancements with a mixture of awe and curiosity, akin to a child discovering a hidden treasure. While they may not be the most tech-savvy individuals, they recognize and appreciate the convenience modern gadgets offer, even as they nostalgically remember the era of rabbit-ear antennas and simpler times.

Sense of Humor: This generation's sense of humor is dry—drier than a martini under the scorching sun of a desert heatwave. They revel in the classic slapstick comedy of Charlie Chaplin, finding boundless amusement in pratfalls, banana peel slips, and the exaggerated physical antics that characterized the silent film era. Their laughter comes easily at the sight of Chaplin's iconic tramp character navigating life's absurdities with his signature blend of grace and clumsiness.

In addition to slapstick, they are aficionados of witty wordplay and clever dialogue, with radio shows like "Fibber McGee and Molly" serving as prime sources of amusement. The rapid-fire banter and sharp, humorous exchanges on these shows tickle their funny bones like a feather duster on speed. They delight in the playful use of language, where puns, double entendres, and clever repartees create a tapestry of humor that is both intelligent and entertaining.

Their humor is often understated, relying on subtlety and nuance rather than overt punchlines. It's a style that requires a keen ear and a quick mind to fully appreciate, and it's this sophisticated approach to comedy that they cherish. Whether it's through the visual gags of early cinema or the verbal dexterity of vintage radio programs, their laughter is a testament to an era where humor was an art form crafted with precision and wit.

Silent Generation (Born 1925–1945)

Taste: The Silent Generation adores food that is as straightforward as a YouTube tutorial for untangling Christmas lights. Their culinary preferences lean towards simple, wholesome dishes that offer comfort and familiarity. They embody the thrifty mindset of a squirrel in a grocery store, ensuring that nothing goes to waste—not even a single grain of rice. Meals are often prepared with an emphasis on frugality and practicality, reflecting the resourcefulness they honed during times of scarcity and economic hardship.

Customs: Having survived the Big Bang of historical chaos, the Silent Generation possesses a remarkable ability to navigate turbulent waters with the stealth and precision of ninjas. They have endured and adapted through numerous societal upheavals, developing a resilience that allows them to remain composed in the face of adversity. Their family secrets are guarded with a level of security that rivals Fort Knox, and their stiff upper lips could give ironing boards a run for their money, showcasing their steadfast determination and stoicism.

Despite their impeccable manners, which are as polished as a freshly pressed tuxedo, the Silent Generation should not be underestimated. Their reserved demeanor can be misleading, as they possess a formidable sense of disapproval. If you cross the line, their "stink eye" has the power to stop a charging rhino dead in its tracks—silent but deadly, their disapproval is unmistakable and intense.

Music: This generation finds joy in the harmonious melodies of doo-wop and the smooth sounds of the Ink Spots. They jive to these classics with the enthusiasm of a pogo stick on springs, embracing the music that defined their youth. Their waltzing skills are so refined and elegant that they can transform any dance party into a royal ball, their movements flowing with grace and precision. For them, music is not just entertainment but a cherished connection to memories of dances and gatherings that brought people together in times of both joy and sorrow.

Technology: They have witnessed an astonishing transformation in technology, from the days of crystal radios to the era of smartphones. While they have adapted impressively to these advancements, the complexities of social media can still baffle them more than a Rubik's cube in the dark. Despite this, they appreciate the convenience and connectivity modern technology offers, even if they occasionally long for the simpler times when communication was more straightforward and personal.

Sense of Humor: The Silent Generation's humor is as arid as a desert in a heatwave, with a dry wit and a love for clever banter. They find mirth in the comedic genius of Bob Hope, laughing as though they've unearthed buried treasure in his sharp one-liners and playful jabs. The escapades of "I Love Lucy" tickle them more than a chorus of hysterical hyenas, as they delight in the timeless humor of Lucy's zany antics and the show's brilliant physical comedy. Their laughter is a blend of nostalgia and appreciation for humor that, like them, has endured the test of time.

Baby Boomers (Born 1946–1964)

Baby Boomers have a deep love for comfort food that evokes a sense of nostalgia, often gravitating towards classic American staples like burgers, fries, and milkshakes. The allure of a classic diner, with its retro ambiance and hearty fare, holds a special place in their hearts. These foods remind them of simpler times and cherished memories from their youth, making every bite a trip down memory lane.

Customs: This generation witnessed monumental changes in the world, from the civil rights movements to the marvels of space exploration. Despite the rapid pace of societal evolution, Baby Boomers tend to uphold cherished traditions. Whether it's gathering the family for Sunday dinner or faithfully tuning in to the evening news, these rituals provide a sense of continuity and stability amidst the whirlwind of change.

Manners: Baby Boomers strike a balance between relaxed manners and a strong emphasis on respect and courtesy. They hold firm to the belief in the power of a handshake and the importance of polite expressions like "please" and "thank you." While they may not adhere to the strict formality of earlier generations, their interactions are characterized by a sincere appreciation for civility and mutual respect.

Music: Having lived through the Beatles' invasion and the iconic Woodstock festival, Baby Boomers' musical tastes are deeply rooted in the sounds of classic rock and Motown. These melodies serve as the anthems of their generation, capturing the spirit and energy of their formative years. Many Boomers still treasure their vinyl collections, with records that tell the story of a musical revolution that defined an era.

Technology: Baby Boomers have witnessed an astonishing evolution in technology, transitioning from rotary phones to smartphones. Though they may not be digital natives, they have shown remarkable adaptability in embracing new technologies. Many Boomers confidently navigate the digital landscape, managing their own Facebook pages and using modern gadgets to stay connected with family and friends.

Sense of Humor: Boomers have a diverse sense of humor, finding joy in both slapstick comedy and sharp-witted humor. They laugh heartily at the antics of "The Three Stooges," enjoying the physical comedy and timeless gags. At the same time, they appreciate the quick wit and insightful humor of comedians like George Carlin, whose clever observations and societal critiques resonate deeply with them. Their laughter is robust and infectious, reflecting a lifetime of finding humor in both the light-hearted and the thought-provoking.

Gen X (Born 1965–1988)

Taste: Generation X has a well-documented love for convenience, often turning to fast food, microwaveable meals, and takeout to suit their busy lifestyles. If convenience were a flavor, they would sprinkle it on everything, even their cereal. Growing up during the rise of fast food chains and ready-made meals, their culinary preferences reflect a blend of practicality and indulgence. They appreciate the speed and ease of grabbing a burger on the go or popping a frozen dinner into the microwave after a long day.

Customs: Raised amidst social and political upheaval, Gen Xers are the quintessential DIY champions. Perfecting the art of being "latchkey kids," they learned to navigate the world with a blend of independence and resourcefulness. Their homes were often run with a cereal box as their secret headquarters, turning everyday items into tools of ingenuity. This generation values self-reliance and has a knack for improvising solutions to life's challenges, a trait honed during their formative years of making do with what was available.

Manners: Gen Xers embrace a casual and relaxed approach to manners, often favoring a friendly nod or a casual greeting over formalities. They are so laid-back that they would probably appreciate a "hey" even if it were delivered via carrier pigeon. Their interactions are marked by a preference for authenticity and straightforwardness, valuing genuine connections over rigid social protocols. This informal style reflects their broader cultural ethos of rejecting pretense and embracing a more down-to-earth way of engaging with others.

Music: Grunge, punk, and hip-hop are the musical anthems that define Generation X. They cherish their Nirvana and Tupac tapes more than their own baby photos, holding onto these relics of their youth with a sense of reverence. For them, music is not just a pastime but a vital part of their identity. They can spin a turntable like it is their own personal DJ booth, reliving the rebellious and transformative sounds that shaped their coming-of-age years. The raw energy and emotional intensity of these genres resonate deeply, capturing the spirit of their generation.

Technology: This generation witnessed the dawn of personal computers and the internet, making them the digital pioneers of the modern era. They navigated the digital jungle with the ease of a tech-savvy ninja, adapting quickly to new technologies and innovations. From the early days of dial-up modems to the proliferation of smartphones, Gen Xers have seen it all and have seamlessly integrated these advancements into their daily lives. Their early exposure to technology has made them adept at troubleshooting and exploring the digital landscape with confidence.

Sense of Humor: Gen Xers have a humor style that is as sarcastic and ironic as a teenager's eye roll. They find amusement in the dry, witty one-liners of "The Simpsons" and the cringe-worthy yet oddly hilarious antics of "The Office." Their sense of humor often reflects a blend of cynicism and wit, poking fun at the absurdities of life with a knowing smirk. This generation appreciates comedy that is smart, irreverent, and unafraid to challenge social norms, finding laughter in both the mundane and the outrageous.

Millennials (Born 1981 - 1996)

Taste: Millennials have elevated the simple act of breakfast into an art form with their love for avocado toast and artisanal coffee. The morning ritual of spreading avocado on toast feels as crucial as cracking a secret code (spoiler: avocado is the key). Their food preferences reflect a desire for health-conscious, aesthetically pleasing meals that often come with a side of social media bragging rights.

Crafting the perfect latte art or discovering the newest superfood is more than just a trend; it's a lifestyle that combines wellness with a touch of gourmet flair.

Customs: Unity, diversity, and sustainability are the core principles that Millennials champion. Their activism game is so strong that they could probably protest their Wi-Fi signal for not being diverse enough. This generation is deeply committed to social justice, environmental causes, and inclusivity, often participating in grassroots movements and digital campaigns. From organizing marches to promoting eco-friendly practices, their customs are shaped by a fervent belief in making the world a better place for everyone.

Manners: Millennials are courteous but prefer to keep things relaxed and approachable. A smile and a hug often replace formal handshakes, reflecting their emphasis on genuine human connection. When it comes to communication, they are as fluent in emojis as they are in English, using digital symbols to convey emotions and add a personal touch to their messages. Their manners strike a balance between respectfulness and informality, creating a friendly and welcoming social environment.

Music: Millennials grew up with a soundtrack of pop, hip-hop, and boy bands that could make their Nintendos jealous. The melodies of Britney Spears and NSYNC transport them back to a time when frosted tips were considered a hairdo masterpiece. Their musical tastes are characterized by a love for catchy, upbeat tunes that evoke nostalgia and a sense of youthful exuberance. Whether it's dancing to the latest pop hit or reminiscing over 90s classics, music plays a significant role in their lives, providing a soundtrack to their experiences and memories.

Technology: This generation is the undisputed ruler of the digital realm, wielding smartphones and social media as their trusty scepters. Having witnessed the internet's birth, they have grown up alongside technology, mastering its various forms and applications. They stream content so frequently that they might as well be living in a town perpetually stuck in "Buffering" mode. From Instagram stories to binge-watching Netflix series, their lives are deeply intertwined with digital connectivity and the latest tech trends.

Sense of Humor: Millennials excel in the art of self-deprecating humor, making them gold medalists if it were an Olympic sport. They revel in internet memes and viral trends, finding humor in the absurdities of life and the quirks of their generation. Their laughter is fueled by the endless content available online, turning everyday struggles into relatable and hilarious moments. It's like living in a never-ending TikTok party where irony, sarcasm, and clever commentary reign supreme.

Gen Z (Born 1997–2011)

Taste: Gen Z's taste buds are adventurous and eclectic, akin to food critics at a circus. They jump from trendy food trucks to customizable bowls faster than a kangaroo on caffeine. Burgers have been swapped out for plant-based dreams and sustainable eating, making Mother Earth their BFF. This generation is all about innovation and health-conscious choices, embracing everything from avocado toast to acai bowls, while always keeping an eye on the latest food trends that are as Instagrammable as they are delicious.

Customs: In the grand parade of life, Gen Z is the one riding a unicycle while juggling bowling balls, constantly challenging norms and redefining conventions. Their online presence is so robust that even the Loch Ness Monster would be jealous. They are digital natives who seamlessly blend virtual and real-world interactions, participating in social media activism, creating viral content, and forging communities that span the globe. Whether it's organizing climate strikes or setting fashion trends, their customs are shaped by a desire for inclusivity, change, and creativity.

Manners: Gen Z is the tech-savvy James Bond of greetings, opting for a casual fist bump over a formal handshake. They communicate through GIFs and emojis that could put the Rosetta Stone to shame, creating a language that's dynamic and expressive. Their manners are informal yet meaningful, valuing authenticity and directness in their interactions. This generation's approach to communication is as fast-paced as their lives, making every interaction efficient and packed with personality.

Music: When not engaged in robot dance-offs, Gen Z grooves to EDM, rap, and pop like it's the dance party of the century. K-pop is their secret weapon, and viral dance challenges are practically their morning workout. Their musical tastes are diverse and global, often influenced by streaming platforms that introduce them to a wide array of genres and artists. Music is not just a pastime but a crucial part of their identity and social life, providing a soundtrack to their daily adventures and virtual hangouts.

Technology: Gen Z and their smartphones are inseparable, like two peas in a pod. They have grown up witnessing the birth of social media, influencer culture, and online activism, making them adept at navigating the digital landscape. If their phone had a pulse, it would probably be their best friend. This generation is always connected, using technology for everything from education to entertainment, and leveraging digital tools to create, share, and advocate for the causes they care about.

Sense of Humor: Their humor is as wild as a squirrel on a sugar rush, built on absurdity, irony, and memes that form the bricks of their digital kingdom. They create viral trends and laugh at online quirks so quirky that even Bigfoot would raise an eyebrow. Their comedic style thrives on quick wit, visual gags, and a deep understanding of internet culture, making their humor both relatable and refreshingly unpredictable. Whether it's a clever TikTok video or a perfectly timed meme, their laughter is a testament to their creativity and unique perspective on the world.

Gen Alpha (Born 2012–present)

Taste: Gen Alpha's foodie adventures are still in beta testing, but they're already gravitating towards snacks that pop with color and pizzazz—meals that are essentially edible toy sets. Picture rainbow-colored fruits, quirky-shaped veggies, and snacks that combine fun with nutrition, making mealtime an experience of play and discovery. Their food choices are influenced by a blend of health-conscious parents and the visual appeal demanded by their vibrant imaginations.

Customs: As the youngest time-travelers of the generational era, Gen Alpha is poised to fill big shoes. They are expected to grow into tech wizards and eco-warriors, practically hatching from their cribs wearing VR headsets. Their customs are still forming, but already they are being shaped by a world that emphasizes sustainability, digital literacy, and global awareness. They participate in virtual classrooms, engage with educational apps, and are introduced early to concepts like recycling and conservation.

Manners: Gen Alpha's manners are in beta testing. They're still deciphering the ancient scrolls of manners, but they're growing up in a world that's more inclusive than a never-ending group hug. Their interactions are marked by a high degree of empathy and acceptance, and they navigate social norms through video chats and virtual reality, which are like their advanced baby talk. Inclusivity and kindness are core to their developing social etiquette, reflecting the values they are being raised with.

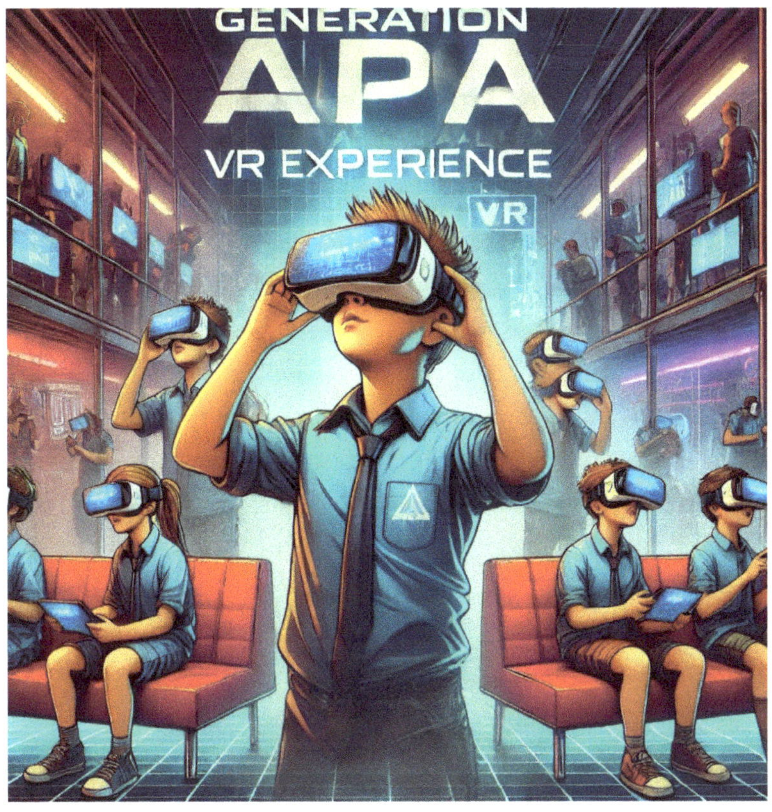

Music: Gen Alpha is composing the soundtrack of the future, a Pandora's playlist yet to be fully unleashed. With streaming services shaping their taste, they'll groove to tunes from every corner of the digital universe. Their musical preferences are influenced by algorithms that introduce them to a vast array of genres and artists, creating a diverse and ever-evolving auditory landscape. Whether it's the latest pop sensation or a classical piece remixed with electronic beats, their music is as varied as the digital world they inhabit.

Technology: Gen Alpha is growing up with tablets and AI devices that might as well be their babysitters. They are more plugged in than a Christmas tree in a light factory, seamlessly interacting with technology from an incredibly young age. From smart toys that respond to their touch to educational apps that teach coding basics, their relationship with technology is intuitive and pervasive. They are the true digital natives, navigating the virtual and physical worlds with equal ease.

Sense of Humor: They're pioneering the "you won't get it" jokes of the future. Their humor is as fresh and evolving as the internet itself, crafting memes and jokes that often leave older generations scratching their heads. They make light of the rapidly changing digital landscape, finding humor in the quirks and idiosyncrasies of their tech-infused reality. As they navigate the ever-shifting virtual cosmos, their comedic sensibilities reflect their unique perspective on a world in constant flux.

9

NOT EVEN IN HOLLYWOOD

In the heart of Hollywood, where dreams were made and fortunes lost with equal abandon, Frank Cutter lived on the edge of it all. He wasn't the star of the show, nor was he even a supporting player. Frank was a freelancing investigative journalist and a paparazzi all in one—a faceless chaser of fame, living in the shadows of those whose lives he desperately sought to capture.

His days blurred into nights as he roamed the glittering streets in search of the story of the century and a shot of a lifetime. Frank's beat-up sedan doubled as his office and his home, a cramped sanctuary from the lavish excesses that surrounded him. It was a stark reminder of broken dreams, a makeshift basecamp from which he waged his nightly campaigns against the facade of Hollywood's high life.

Tonight, however, would be different. It was a balmy summer evening when Frank staked out Belle Étoile Brasserie, an elegant restaurant nestled in an upscale Hollywood neighborhood. The place was a magnet for celebrities—actors, musicians, and socialites—who dined under the soft glow of chandeliers, oblivious to the man lurking in the shadows with his camera.

From his vantage point amidst carefully manicured bushes across the street, Frank observed the lively scene unfolding inside. Through the large windows, he could see the opulent interior adorned with crystal chandeliers casting warm, golden light over linen-clad tables. Waiters in crisp uniforms glided effortlessly between guests, carrying trays of delicate hors d'oeuvres and sparkling glasses of champagne.

Outside, the evening took on a surreal quality as the Hollywood Hills loomed in the distance, their silhouettes softened by the city lights below. Stretch limousines lined the curbs, disgorging elegantly dressed patrons who entered the restaurant with an air of effortless sophistication. Paparazzi like Frank hovered in the shadows, their cameras poised for any glimpse of celebrity glamour that might spill onto the sidewalk.

As Philip St. Clair emerged from the restaurant, followed closely by his sous chef, Darius, Frank saw his chance. He snapped photo after photo, hoping to catch Philip in a compromising position—a secret rendezvous, a heated argument, anything that would sell to the tabloids.

"You can't keep underpaying me like this, Philip." Darius's voice carried a hint of frustration as they stepped onto the sidewalk, away from the prying eyes of the restaurant's guests.

Philip glanced around nervously, unaware of Frank's presence in the shadows. "Keep your voice down, Darius. We can't afford any more scandals," he replied in a hushed tone, trying to maintain composure.

"I don't care about your scandals, Philip. I've had enough!" Darius's voice rose slightly, drawing curious glances from nearby patrons entering the restaurant.

"You think you can threaten me here?" Philip's tone turned sharp, his face darkening with anger. "Remember who made you what you are today."

Frank strained to capture every word, his camera clicking silently as the confrontation escalated. This was the moment he had been waiting for—the crack in Philip St. Clair's polished facade.

Hours passed. Frank remained hidden in the shadows, nursing a lukewarm cup of coffee from a nearby convenience store. The night grew colder, and the streets emptied of the glamorous facades that defined Hollywood's allure. Just as Frank contemplated calling it a night, a figure emerged from the darkness.

A hooded silhouette approached Frank's hiding spot, moving with purposeful steps that sent a chill down his spine. Before Frank could react, the figure lunged at him, a flash of metal glinting in the dim streetlight. Pain exploded in Frank's chest as he staggered backward, his camera clattering to the pavement.

Gasping for breath, Frank saw the glint of recognition in his assailant's eyes—a fleeting moment of shock and regret before the figure disappeared into the night. The last thing Frank heard was the distant wail of sirens and the echoing footsteps of onlookers rushing to his aid.

Detective Beth Hayes arrived at the crime scene—a stark contrast to the glamour she associated with Hollywood. Frank's lifeless body lay sprawled on the pavement, surrounded by flashing police lights and curious bystanders. She kneeled beside him, noting the fatal wound and the scattered remnants of his equipment.

"He was a journalist," her partner, Detective Ramirez, remarked grimly.

Hayes nodded, her gaze scanning the area for clues. Frank's murder had sent shockwaves through the community, casting suspicion on those whose lives he had relentlessly pursued. Philip St. Clair, in particular, had become the focal point of gossip and speculation—an unexpected twist in his rise to culinary fame. Rumor had it that the celebrity chef was an impostor, and his magazine-worthy creations were stolen from his sous chef, Darius. Frank was on the verge of uncovering it all and unmasking one of Hollywood's famous.

Despite their suspicions, Hayes and Ramirez lacked concrete evidence linking Philip to the crime. Hollywood's elite closed ranks, shielding their own from the prying eyes of justice. Meanwhile, Philip's world unraveled as the scandal tarnished his reputation and drove away patrons from his once-thriving restaurant.

Months passed, and Philip St. Clair found himself adrift in a sea of adversity. His restaurant, once a beacon of culinary excellence, stood empty and forlorn. The whispers of Frank's murder lingered like a ghost, haunting Philip's every step as he wandered the streets of Hollywood, homeless and broken.

No longer the celebrated chef, Philip became a shadow of his former self—a man stripped of his wealth and influence, reduced to seeking shelter in abandoned corners and forgotten alleys. Hunger gnawed at his stomach, and the cold nights offered no solace from the harsh realities of his downfall.

Evening after evening, Philip found himself wandering the streets that kept drawing him back to his former restaurant, now under new ownership. He stared at it from afar, reminiscing about the high life he once lived and the fame he had enjoyed. The security guard at the front door, not recognizing who he was beyond another dirty homeless man ruining the image of Hollywood, sent him away. He limped into the shadows, resigning himself to the fact that he wouldn't be able to ease his hunger.

Desperately seeking shelter among the parked cars along the sidewalk, he tried each handle with cautious hope. As rain began to fall, he continued his hopeless search until he stumbled upon an abandoned car tucked away in a secluded alley. Desperation clawed at him as he eyed the vehicle, its windows cracked, and its interior darkened by neglect.

With trembling hands, Philip forced open the car door, hoping to find refuge from the unforgiving streets and the heavy rainfall. But as he settled into the cramped space, his eyes fell upon remnants of a life left behind—empty food containers, scattered clothing. Philip examined each artifact with care and set aside the items he could use later. He flipped through the scattered photographs that lay strewn across the worn-out seat. Each photograph depicted moments captured in time: a bustling red carpet event, candid shots of celebrities laughing over dinner, and discreet images of whispered conversations in shadowy corners. As Philip sifted through the memories frozen in those pictures, a sense of recognition crept over him.

Among the photographs, he found several portraits of Frank Cutter himself, often in the background, discreetly capturing the essence of Hollywood's elite. Philip's breath caught as he realized where he was sitting—in Frank's car, the very man whose relentless pursuit to expose him cost him his life.

Philip's thoughts swirled in a tumultuous storm of regret and realization as he sat in the car, grappling with the weight of Frank Cutter's legacy and the consequences of his own actions. The rain drummed steadily on the car roof, a relentless reminder of the night's somber atmosphere. Seeking solace or perhaps seeking atonement, Philip reached out and turned on the car radio.

The soft jazz provided Philip with a fleeting moment of solace, only to be interrupted by the start of the midnight news. "Tonight, the murdered journalist Frank Cutter was awarded a posthumous Pulitzer Prize for his exposé on Hollywood's disgraced chef, Philip St. Clair," the announcer's voice filled the quiet car. "Frank Cutter's notes, crucial evidence in the case, were found in a lockbox at Highland Station, leading to his recognition in journalism.

Despite being cleared of any criminal wrongdoing, the scandal surrounding Philip St. Clair has left his restaurant empty and his whereabouts unknown."

As the radio host's voice faded into the background, Philip St. Clair realized that the city, where dreams were made and shattered with equal measure, had imprisoned him for eternity, while lifting Frank into the limelight.

10

GESTATIONAL IMPACT STATEMENT

Marcus H. for Roe v. Wade

Dear Justices of the United States Supreme Court

I had not intended to file a victim impact statement, but in light of the details I learned on June 24, 2022, I feel compelled to tell the court my side of the story.

My name will be Marcus when I am born, but I am only six weeks along, and my mother has not yet discovered that she is pregnant. I am only the size of a pea and look more like a tadpole than the handsome, well-established, stable, and successful man you hope I will grow into.

Christie, my mother, is a twenty-year-old brunette and a budding hairstylist with boundless ambition and high expectations for the future. She currently resides in Georgia, but after graduating from beauty school, she plans to relocate to California to pursue her dream of becoming a film hairstylist. She needs to take a huge leap of faith to achieve her lofty dreams because of her current circumstances. But for my mother, staying with her abusive father and living just above the poverty line is far less comforting than going into the unknown.

One evening, when her friends invited her out for a well-deserved night out, she said yes. She laughed and danced, enjoying a rare moment of joy. When a friend of a friend offered to drive her home at the end of the night, she accepted, thinking it was a kind gesture. Unfortunately, he thought her need for a ride also gave him the right to rape her. I am sure you would not do such a thing, but that guy did. I am confident the Weinsteins and Epsteins did not think their assaults were rape, but this is my moment, and I would digress.

Every time my mother is alone with her thoughts, she will relive the rape all over again. She will not be able to put it down, shrug it off, or leave it behind. She will remember how she cried, fought, pleaded, and bargained, but she had been physically and mentally subdued and had lost the battle. "It'd be over sooner if you didn't fight," my soon-to-be father said.

She will be devastated when she sees the positive line on the test weeks later, but her future will freeze in time when she gets a glimpse of the speckle of dust on the ultrasound machine's screen, confirming I am not a false positive. However, she received more than me as a parting gift. It will take a few more weeks before she finds out that her rapist also gave her gonorrhea. Two for the price of one—what a steal!

The state's denial of my mother's right to an abortion will cause her despair to worsen. "Let that baby live." "A heartbeat can be heard." "It is God's creation." You will say, but for fuck's sake, it was her asshole rapist's work, not God's. We are a little smarter than to believe in the immaculate conception, and anyone who says that God wanted my mother to be raped is insane, because it all starts there. However, you justify my existence afterward.

My mother will hate me as I grow inside her because I will always remind her of how her body was violated, her mental health was taken away, and her dreams were crushed in a matter of minutes.

"You'll bond," you will say. "You can put the baby up for adoption," you will recommend. Everyone will have advice, but no one will offer a plan or lend a hand for how she can get her life back after such devastation. My father said, "It'd be over sooner if you didn't fight." But it won't end there—not in the next nine months, and not ever! How do you not get that?

After enduring eighteen hours of labor, I will be delivered on a Monday night in February. President's Day. What a vision! The nurse will place me on her chest. My mother will cry, but not because of the Hallmark moment of happiness as we collectively reach for tissues. No. She will be mourning her hopes. Her life. You will have saved me. Congratulations.

My mother will not give me up for adoption. Not because she will bond with me on a visceral and unconditional level, but because her father will make her get on welfare. She will never go back to school, but she will spend hundreds of thousands of dollars raising me until I reach adulthood, working several jobs. The rapist will not pay. The government will help a little, but she will barely notice it. Where are you now?

My mother's invisible trauma will cover us like the Emperor's New Clothes for the rest of our miserable lives. She is a victim of sexual assault, and I am the memory she will want to erase. My body will bear obvious signs of this hidden sorrow, and I will become the rapist who victimized my mother. She will not let go of her hatred for me or the numerous violent partners who preyed on her wounded psyche. The once-beautiful girl, dreaming of flying high and making it big, will slowly degenerate into a broken, wounded bird not worth saving. Survival of the fittest. Do not fuck with nature.

By my sixteenth birthday, I will be in and out of juvie for stealing and dealing drugs, and by twenty, I will have committed my first murder. I will spend my whole life feeling unwanted by anyone I want to love me. My mother, society, but above all, me. I will hate myself for ruining my mother's life. But will it really be me, or will it be you?

Your plan will work. I will still be here, but is this the life you have planned for me? Or will you intend for me to be adopted by a white, devout, minivan-driving family in the hope that I will never come to know that I will be the child of a rapist? When you signed the document overturning Roe v. Wade, you did not say what you had in mind for all women and daughters. You prevented my mother from aborting me, but you should have let her. I may not know any better, but my mother would.

As I stand accused of multiple murders, the judge will hand me the death sentence at the age of twenty-one, but you—you ended my mother's life by allowing me to live; but at the end of the day, you will kill me anyway. You play one twisted God.

II

A POKER PLAYER'S TALE

In the dimly lit world of high-stakes poker, where fortunes could change in a single hand, Bill navigated a life filled with uncertainty. Born with epilepsy, he faced the unpredictability of seizures that could strike at any moment. It was a condition that might have sidelined him from the poker world altogether, but he had a secret weapon—a four-legged companion named Ace, a mature Border Collie.

Ace was more than just a loyal dog; he was a highly trained service animal. His keen senses allowed him to predict Bill's seizures before they occurred. With a subtle nudge or a particular bark, Ace could signal Bill, giving him just enough time to withdraw from a game and prevent a public episode. The bond between Bill and Ace began several years ago when Ace was a puppy and Bill was stepping out of the confines of his home to make a name for himself in the card game world.

In the competitive world of poker, Bill was often dismissed as an underdog. His unassuming appearance and battle with epilepsy made him an unlikely contender. He resembled a bank teller straight out of the eighties—beige everything, no tattoos, no shiny sweatpants, sunglasses, or attitude. He was as dull as the color he wore.

The duo began their journey in low-stakes games, working their way up the ladder. Bill's game stagnated for a few years before improving rapidly, drawing attention and skepticism from opponents and fans alike. But he remained the underdog, and everyone loves an underdog.

The pinnacle of all tournaments was the World Series of Poker, where the best gathered to compete for the champion's title, and Bill had his sights set on this prestigious event. It was a dream that had eluded him for years, but with each tournament, he inched closer, making this dream a reality. He wanted to prove to the world and all those who had ridiculed him, that he was the number one player.

As the World Series approached, the pressure mounted, but Bill's seizures remained under control. The competition was fierce, filled with seasoned professionals who would stop at nothing to claim victory. Bill ranked last among 8,569 participants, but over several days, he steadily navigated through 67 tables before gaining any recognition.

The final table was a tense affair. The atmosphere crackled with electric energy, and the stakes were higher than ever. Alongside Bill sat eight notable players, each bringing their A-game to claim victory. The most favored among bettors was "Stone-faced" Felix Marino, sporting several championship rings on his fingers. Felix rarely showed emotion, earning him the nickname "Stone-Faced." His unwavering focus and stoic demeanor made it difficult for opponents to read his next move.

Then there was "Rapid" Rick Riley, the Speedster, known for lightning-fast decisions. He analyzed hands swiftly, often catching opponents off guard. The most colorful character was "Prof. Bluff" Lawrence Pemberton, at 70, the oldest player to reach the final table. Lawrence, with his background in psychology, read everyone like an open book, mastering psychological warfare.

And, of course, Helen Lovelace, "The Heartbreaker," the only lady at the table, was a master manipulator who used charm to lead opponents into emotional decisions. And then there was Bill.

He sat in silence in his beige polyester polo shirt, buttoned all the way up, hair slightly greasy—certainly not television material. The players ignored him completely as they joked around. He was nothing but a ghost, and except for Ace by his side, no one cared.

The plays were tense, but even—every player won and lost some. Bill, with his dull bank teller-like demeanor, grew restless as the game dragged on, while others relished their time in the spotlight. The dealer dealt the cards, and the first round of betting began with "Rapid" Rick Riley, who placed a modest bet without hesitation.

"Prof. Bluff" Thompson and Bill called, while "Stone-faced" Felix Marino raised the stakes. Miller, Lee, and Davis folded, and Helen "The Heartbreaker," holding a Two of Diamonds and a Five of Clubs, followed suit. With four players remaining, the tension mounted. The dealer revealed the flop: Five of Spades, Four of Spades, and Ten of Clubs.

Marino, with an Ace of Clubs and Seven of Clubs, anticipated a potential flush, raising the stakes. Bill and Riley stayed in the game, matching his bet, while Thompson hesitated before calling.

The turn revealed a Two of Diamonds, improving Riley's flush odds. Bill held a Ten of Spades and a Jack of Diamonds, boasting the strongest hand with a pair of Tens. "Prof. Bluff" Thompson displayed a confident smirk, suggesting a strong hand. The room buzzed with tension. Thompson still held a pair of Nines, while "Stone-faced" Felix Marino and Riley pinned their hopes on the river.

Just as the final bets were placed, Ace emitted a low growl and scratched his ear. Bill glanced over and gently petted him, while his opponents watched, annoyed and waiting to see if Bill would suffer an episode, potentially halting the game. Bill hesitated, then made a bold move, pushing all his chips to the center. All in. The pot surged to a record $8 million.

His rivals raised their eyebrows, taken aback. They couldn't allow this unknown player to humiliate them in such a high-stakes event. The room pulsed with tension as the final card, the Eight of Hearts, was revealed.

"Stone-faced" Felix Marino's face drained of color as he slowly revealed his cards—a failed flush. Thompson remained strong with a pair of Nines, while Riley managed a pair of Eights—strong hands, but not strong enough to beat Bill's pair of Tens. The room held its breath. Spectators exchanged confused glances, but Marino, Thompson, and Riley knew Bill had won the World Series of Poker, defying all odds and expectations.

Bill basked in newfound fame and fortune as Ace remained faithfully by his side. Yet, as accolades poured in and the spotlight shone brightly on him, his rivals couldn't accept defeat at the hands of the "Beige Man," as they called him.

In a private moment, Bill gazed into Ace's eyes. The loyal dog wagged his tail with pure joy. Ace wasn't just a service dog who predicted seizures. Over the years, Bill had trained him to count cards and signal sophisticated cues, aiding his strategic plays at the table. Each scratch, growl, and bark held significance that fooled rivals and the world alike.

12

THE RECIPE

If you watched the news on January 6, 2021, you know how deliciously fake news pairs with a former president and the pungent existential crisis of masculinity. I feel this heartfelt remake of this complex disaster goes a long way, but if you watch your future, you do not go for seconds.

The Insurgency Bowl

Serves: Several million
Cooking Level: Advanced
Cuisine: Uniquely American
Cooking Time: Decades

Ingredients:

- About a thousand angry people
- Freshly ground weapon of your choice
- Fake news

- Shredded, pickled Masculinity *
- Granulated Hatred
- Thinly sliced #MeToo movement
- Distilled white Racism
- Reduced sodium Equality
- Bible salt to taste
- Spicy premium Sexism
- Cooked Democracy

*Ensure that this product is not rage-free if you do not want to pickle your own masculinity crisis.

Instructions:

Step 1. Prepare the Meat:
Season the metaphorical "meat" with Bible salt and the freshly ground weapon of your choice. This sets the stage for the simmering tension and conflict to come. Allow it to marinate while preparing the other ingredients.

Step 2. Mix the Political Mixture:
In a symbolic bowl, combine fake news, granulated hatred, and distilled racism. These ingredients represent the volatile ideological mix that fuels societal divisions. Pour this mixture over the metaphorical "meat" and let it soak in, intensifying the flavors of discontent.

Step 3. Simmering Resentment:
Place the seasoned crowd in the symbolic pressure cooker of Capitol Hill. This step symbolizes the gathering storm of discontent and frustration that culminates in a public display of unrest. Reserve the simmering sauce of societal tensions for later use.

Step 4. Pickled Masculinity:
Extract the essence of masculinity, pickling it in the context of
#MeToo movements and calls for equality. This step reflects evolv-
ing societal expectations and challenges to traditional gender roles.
Let it mature over time, amplifying its impact.

Step 5. Serving Democracy:
Present cooked democracy in a fragile serving bowl, sprinkling it
with a touch of spicy sexism to highlight ongoing gender biases.
Top it with a portion of angry people, symbolizing public discontent, and drizzle it with the now thickened sauce of fake news,
hatred, and racism from the pressure cooker.

Step 6. Garnish with Controversy:
Finally, garnish each serving with controversy. Served on January
6, 2021.

13

THE FINAL BOW

Guillette the Great stood stoically on the worn wooden stage, his piercing gaze locked on the hollow eyes of a human skull. The spotlight bathed him in an eerie glow, casting shadows that danced like specters around him. The audience held their collective breath, anticipation palpable in the air, as if the very essence of mystery itself had materialized before them.

As an illusionist of unparalleled renown, Guillette had spent his entire career traversing the ethereal realms, beckoning forth the spirits of the departed. Kings and queens of bygone eras, heroes of medieval battles, and even the illustrious Julius Caesar himself graced his stage. His performances were legendary, his prowess unmatched, and his entourage was extravagant.

The world adored him, enraptured by the enigmatic aura that enveloped him whenever he appeared in public. His signature long black topcoat billowed around him, his jet-black hair swept back with precision, and a meticulously groomed mustache lent him an air of sophistication that belied his humble origins. Born Hans Wagner in Berlin to a butcher and his wife, he had adopted the persona of Guillette the Great after a spectral visitor foretold his destiny at the tender age of sixteen—a destiny that would elevate him to the pinnacle of illusionary artistry by the age of forty.

Yet, behind the curtain of his public persona, Guillette harbored a profound ambivalence toward his admirers and an abiding contempt for his detractors. Social interactions unsettled him; he found solace and kinship among the spirits that populated his world of shadows and secrets.

In his youth, he commanded the dead effortlessly—they appeared at his summons and retreated at his bidding. But with time, they grew capricious, appearing uninvited and departing at their own whim. Their unpredictability only fueled Guillette's mystique, drawing him deeper into a world where reality blurred with illusion. For decades, he traversed continents, performing for cheering crowds, dignitaries, and skeptical heads of state alike.

But now, as the twilight of his career approached, Guillette felt the weight of years and ailments. A goiter and a bout of syphilis contracted in the exotic Orient had left his health fragile, despite the doctor's prescriptions of iodine applied with caution. The time had come to hang his topcoat and bid farewell to the stage that had been his kingdom.

Tonight was his grand finale, the culmination of a lifetime spent weaving magic and mystery into the fabric of reality. Tickets had sold out months in advance, and the theater was packed to capacity with eager spectators yearning to witness one last marvel from the master.

GUILLETE
THE GREAT
GUILLETE THE GREAT
GUILLETE THE GREAT

As the curtains parted and darkness enveloped the stage, a hush fell over the audience, their collective breath held in suspense. Guillette stood alone, gazing into the empty sockets of the skull before him. In a frenzied soliloquy, he beseeched the spirits to join him one final time, their voices clamoring for attention in the fading twilight of his career. The performance was electrifying, poignant—a testament to a lifetime of mastery and devotion.

When the final curtain fell and the applause thundered through the theater, Guillette took his last bow—a gesture befitting a monarch of his craft. The heavy red velvet muffled the sounds of adulation as he collapsed and died on stage, the curtain descending on his final act.

"Accidental iodine poisoning," the coroner concluded a few days later.

"No foul play," the police said, and the world mourned the loss of its greatest.

A year before, in Zurich, after another successful sold-out night, a man from the audience approached Guillette. He introduced himself as Dr. Eugen Bleule, a Swiss psychiatrist who had followed Guillette's career for years. Dr. Bleule told him he most likely suffered from schizophrenia and offered a consult. Suddenly, everything that ever made sense to Guillette was no longer providing comfort, and he felt as if everyone he ever cared for had abandoned him at once.

The spirit of Guillette The Great died in the dim dressing room in Switzerland that night as Hans Wagner realized he was not the greatest showman the world had ever seen.

14

EEYORE'S REFLECTIVE RETELLINGS OF FAMOUS QUOTES

Eyore, with his perpetually droopy demeanor and a disposition that often hovers between gloomy and resigned, has a unique way of interpreting the world around him. His take on famous quotes often reflects his thoughtful but melancholic nature. If Eeyore retold famous quotes, they might have a whiff of doubt and a dash of melancholy, but hidden in the shadows of his words is a subtle wisdom. His retellings infuse these historical phrases with a dose of his own endearing pessimism, offering a perspective that is both uniquely Eeyore and unexpectedly insightful.

American Declaration of Independence (1776):

Thomas Jefferson: *"We hold these truths to be self-evident, that all men are created equal, that they are endowed by their Creator with certain unalienable Rights, that among these are Life, Liberty and the pursuit of Happiness."*

Eeyore: "Well, um, it's like we're supposed to believe that everyone's the same and, uh, that we're given these rights that no one can take away. But, you know, life can be a bit tricky, liberty feels a bit fleeting, and as for happiness, well, it seems to be playing hide and seek with me most of the time. At least Pooh, Piglet, and the others make it a bit easier to find now and then."

French Revolution (1789):

Maximilien Robespierre: *"Liberty, equality, fraternity."*

Eeyore: "Um, liberty sounds nice, but it's, uh, not always as free as they say. And equality—well, that seems a bit hard to find sometimes. Fraternity? Oh, bother, that's a tall order in a world where everyone seems to be in their own little rain cloud."

The Women's Suffrage Movement (early 20th century):

Although not directly related to the suffrage movement, the quote has been associated with the spirit of independence and empowerment embraced by the movement.

Charlotte Brontë: *"I am no bird, and no net ensnares me; I am a free human being with an independent will."*

Eeyore: "Oh, well, I'm not exactly a bird, but I don't feel entirely free either. It's like, um, being stuck in some invisible net, you know? I'm trying to be independent, but, uh, the world's a bit tangled most of the time. Pooh tries to help me out, though, even if we both get a bit lost sometimes."

The Treaty of Versailles (1919):

Marshal Ferdinand Foch, a French military commander, expressed skepticism about the long-term prospects of peace after World War I.

Marshal Ferdinand Foch: *"This is not a peace treaty. It is an armistice for twenty years."*

Eeyore: "Well, it's not quite the peace we hope for. More like a little break, you know, for about twenty years. After that, well, who knows what gloomy clouds might gather again?"

World War II (1939–1945):

The U.S. President said in his speech to Congress after the attack on Pearl Harbor:

Franklin D. Roosevelt: *"Yesterday, December 7, 1941, a date which will live in infamy..."*

Eeyore: "Well, yesterday was, um, December 7, 1941, a day that, uh, everyone will remember for, um, not very good reasons. Just like most days, really, full of clouds and not much sunshine."

The Cuban Missile Crisis (1962):

John F. Kennedy: *"We will not prematurely or unnecessarily risk the costs of worldwide nuclear war in which even the fruits of victory would be ashes in our mouth; but neither will we shrink from that risk at any time it must be faced."*

Eeyore: "Well, we wouldn't want to rush into something so, um, gloomy and dreadful like a worldwide nuclear war. But if it comes to that, well, we'll have to face it, won't we? It's just another storm cloud looming over us."

Moon Landing (1969):

Neil Armstrong: *"That's one small step for [a] man, one giant leap for mankind."*

Eeyore: "Well, it's a tiny step for someone, I suppose. But, um, a huge leap for everyone else. Not that it matters much in the grand scheme of gloomy things. Still, I suppose Pooh would say it's an adventure worth taking."

The Watergate Scandal (1972–1974):

Press conference addressing the allegations surrounding the Watergate scandal.

Richard Nixon: *"I'm not a crook."*

Eeyore: "Oh, I'm not quite sure if I'm a crook or not. Maybe someone else can tell, but, um, I hope not. Though, you know, things seem to go awry around here sometimes."

"I Have a Dream" Speech (1963):

Martin Luther King Jr.: *"I have a dream that one day this nation will rise up and live out the true meaning of its creed: 'We hold these truths to be self-evident: that all men are created equal.'"*

Eeyore: "I, uh, have a dream too, but sometimes dreams seem a bit far away. Maybe one day we'll all be equal, but until then, it's a lot of waiting and hoping in the rain."

Fall of the Berlin Wall (1989):

Ronald Reagan: *"Mr. Gorbachev, tear down this wall!"*

Eeyore: "Well, Mr. Gorbachev, if you wouldn't mind, maybe you could, um, think about, you know, tearing down that wall. But if not, well, I suppose we'll manage somehow. Pooh would probably say we can climb over it together."

Inaugural Address (1961):

John F. Kennedy: *"Ask not what your country can do for you—ask what you can do for your country."*

Eeyore: "Well, I suppose it's a good idea to think about what you can do for your country, even if, uh, it might not always do much for you in return. Just another one of those things, I guess."

Release of Nelson Mandela (1990):

Nelson Mandela: *"I have cherished the ideal of a democratic and free society in which all persons live together in harmony and with equal opportunities."*

Eeyore: "Well, it's a lovely ideal, living together in harmony and all. But, um, sometimes harmony feels a bit like a distant dream. Equal opportunities sound nice, too, if they weren't so hard to find."

September 11 Attacks (2001):

George W. Bush: *"Terrorist attacks can shake the foundations of our biggest buildings, but they cannot touch the foundation of America."*

Eeyore: "Well, those attacks were, um, very shaking indeed. But I suppose, deep down, there's something in us that they can't quite reach, even if it feels like the world is tumbling down around us."

15

LEGACY

The first bullet went to Ms. Rappaport, Connor's revered chemistry teacher. He hesitated, holding his breath, contemplating who should follow. The room, once alive with Ms. Rappaport's vibrant teaching, now hung in an unsettling silence.

Ms. Rappaport had been a cornerstone of Hillside High School in serene Willowbrook, Vermont, for decades. Her dedication to education extended far beyond academics; she was a beacon of inspiration and a beloved figure in the community. With a heart as expansive as the Vermont sky, she transformed the challenge of chemistry into an exhilarating journey for her students. Her classroom wasn't just about learning formulas; it was a place where young minds discovered their potential. Students adored her, and colleagues held her in high esteem.

Despite Hillside High's small size, Ms. Rappaport's laboratory was a marvel—a testament to her commitment. It housed top-notch equipment, a treasure trove of scientific knowledge that fueled curiosity and nurtured intellect. She spared no effort in ensuring that every student who passed through her classroom had access to top-notch resources, igniting their curiosity and nurturing their intellectual growth.

Willowbrook, Vermont, was a tranquil town ensconced between the meandering Otter Creek and the gentle rolling hills, an idyllic backdrop for nature enthusiasts and those seeking a quiet, peaceful life. It was a place where nothing ever happened, and that is precisely the way its residents preferred it. For the occasional fishermen and curious travelers who passed through, Willowbrook was a hidden gem, known for its charm and its enduring sense of community.

Willowbrook, nestled between Otter Creek and gentle hills, cherished its quietude. Ms. Rappaport embodied the town's spirit—not just as a teacher but as a core part of its identity. Her warmth and dedication to teaching extended beyond the classroom; she believed in nurturing both minds and communities.

Through the years, Ms. Rappaport has touched the lives of countless students, imparting not just knowledge but also life lessons. She often said, "Chemistry isn't just about elements and compounds; it's about connections and reactions. Just as in life, it's the bonds we form and how we react to situations that define who we are."

Connor, one of her senior students, was a troubled soul. He had walked into her classroom with a chip on his shoulder and a disinterest in science. Ms. Rappaport, however, saw potential in him that he could not see in himself. She mentored him, patiently guiding him through the intricacies of chemistry while offering a sympathetic ear for his struggles outside the classroom.

Connor, once a troubled senior with a disinterest in science, found an unexpected mentor in Ms. Rappaport. Raised amidst turmoil—an abusive father and distant mother—he carried burdens that weighed heavily. At Hillside High, his peers added to his struggles, subjecting him to ridicule and bullying. Yet, Ms. Rappaport's unwavering belief in him and her ability to connect slowly broke through his defenses.

In time, Connor immersed himself in the world of elements and atoms, guided by Ms. Rappaport's patient mentorship. Her words echoed: personal growth, like a chemical reaction, required patience, dedication, and the right catalyst—qualities she embodied for him.

One day, while exploring the depths of the chemistry lab, Connor stumbled upon Ms. Rappaport's journals. Among the notes on experiments and research were personal reflections on teaching and life. A particular entry caught his eye: "My greatest joy is seeing my students flourish, but my deepest wish is for them to pay it forward, spreading knowledge, kindness, and compassion to the world. A single bullet, aimed at changing lives for the better, can have a profound impact."

Connor was deeply moved by this revelation, and the words weighed heavily on his conscience. The "single bullet" in the journal was a metaphor, but he could not shake the idea that he was meant to carry the torch of Ms. Rappaport's legacy.

On that cold winter day, as Connor sat in her classroom, contemplating who should be next, he realized that there was no one else who had such a profound impact on his life. Ms. Rappaport's influence had been an enduring force for good, and he was determined to honor her dedication as she prepared for retirement.

He looked around the eerily quiet classroom, and with renewed purpose, Connor deleted the next bullet from his college admission essay. Instead, he emphasized his commitment to pursuing chemical engineering at the Massachusetts Institute of Technology, driven by Ms. Rappaport's dedication and the impact she had on his life.

16

HAPPY HOUR

It's 5 o'clock somewhere.

In the dim glow of an old-fashioned bar, where time seemed to pause and every drink held a tale, a diverse cast of characters gathered each evening, each with their own unique passion for their chosen elixir. From the suave Dirty Martini Devotees to the spirited Margarita Maniacs, the bar was a microcosm of eclectic enthusiasts, each sip transporting them to different worlds. Here, amidst the hum of conversations and the clinking of glasses, stories unfolded, creating a rich tapestry of life, laughter, and libations, where every cocktail was a portal to a different era, adventure, or dream.

Old Fashioned Enthusiasts

These individuals are like modern-day time travelers, convinced that sipping on an Old Fashioned teleports them to a bygone era when people wore monocles and had an unshakable obsession with top hats. You'll spot them at the bar, earnestly ordering their drink as if they're about to embark on a genteel journey through Victorian London, complete with dramatic exclamations of "Good sir, another round of Old Fashioneds, if you please!" Their enthusiasm for this classic cocktail is so infectious that you might find yourself yearning for a pocket watch and a fondness for waxed mustaches by the time you finish your drink.

Dirty Martini Devotees

These aficionados of the olive-infused elixir consider themselves the James Bonds of the drinking world.

With each sip of their dirty martini, they are convinced they are stepping into the shoes of a suave, sophisticated secret agent on a mission to save the world—though it is more likely they are just saving themselves from another mundane evening.

Watch as they casually twirl their cocktail picks, savoring each olive as if it holds the key to a hidden spy network. You might even catch them checking their watches and scanning the room for imaginary adversaries, all while exuding an air of unparalleled sophistication, shaken, not stirred.

Cosmopolitan Sippers

If you suspect you have stumbled into a real-life episode of "Sex and the City" when you see someone ordering a Cosmo, you have probably encountered one of these aficionados. For them, drinking a Cosmo is like rewatching the series and fervently hoping it still holds up in the modern world, much like their collection of fashion magazines from the early 2000s. These enthusiasts likely have a closet bursting at the seams with designer shoes, most of which are too precarious to walk in but too fabulous to resist. They also possess an uncanny ability to weave puns into any conversation, as if puns were the Manolo Blahniks of the linguistic world—stylish, attention-grabbing, and occasionally painful if overused.

Daiquiri Die-Hards

These eternal optimists are firm believers that a Daiquiri can whisk them away to an eternal beach vacation, even if they are just sipping it in a landlocked suburb. Watch as they take their optimism to the next level, often accessorizing their drink with tiny umbrellas, miniature surfboards, and a collection of plastic flamingos—because nothing says "I'm on a beach" like a plastic flamingo on your cocktail glass. Their dedication to the Daiquiri is so unwavering that you might even catch them doing a hula dance or humming tropical tunes, completely transported to a beach they've never visited.

Margarita Maniacs

These enthusiastic margarita lovers are like walking fiestas, always ready to party. They firmly subscribe to the notion that tequila, salt, and lime hold the keys to life, as if those ingredients are the secret to unlocking eternal happiness. Their motto? "Why have one when you can have three?" These aficionados view a trio of margaritas not as a sign of overindulgence but as a well-thought-out life strategy. You will often find them embellishing their drinks with elaborate salt rims, garnishing them with enough lime wedges to start a fruit stand, and proclaiming that "Margaritaville" should be the national anthem. Expect spontaneous salsa dancing and a never-ending supply of sombreros whenever they're around; they're a fiesta in human form!

Manhattan Mavens

These Manhattan enthusiasts are the self-proclaimed intellectuals of the cocktail world. They approach their drink with the gravitas of someone pondering life's deepest mysteries in a dimly lit café. Sipping a Manhattan for them is like savoring a fine Shakespearean soliloquy or decoding ancient hieroglyphs—profound, complex, and occasionally baffling to those nearby. If you ever find yourself in need of existential advice, they're your go-to philosophers. Just be prepared for a discussion that weaves seamlessly from the meaning of life to the merits of rye whiskey.

They are the type to quote Shakespeare while stirring their Manhattan and might even insist that the cocktail's cherry garnish is a metaphor for the fleeting nature of human existence.

Mojito Masters

These eternal optimists and Mojito aficionados firmly believe that muddled mint and a dash of lime can cure any ailment, from a bad day at work to a broken heart. They are the living embodiment of the "Keep calm and carry on" mantra, interpreting it as "Keep calm and shake that Mojito." Watch in awe as they muddle mint leaves with the precision of a surgeon and zest limes with the finesse of a concert pianist. For them, a Mojito is not just a drink; it is a potion for invincibility, an elixir that transforms life's lemons into zest for their favorite cocktail. You might even catch them whispering sweet words to their mint leaves, convinced that positive affirmations enhance the flavor. They are the kind of optimists who, after a Mojito or two, believe they can conquer the world—starting with the garden where they grow their mint.

Bloody Mary Buffs

These ardent devotees of the Bloody Mary have an unwavering faith in the miraculous healing powers of vodka, tomato juice, and an entire salad skewered on a stick. They regard this "brunch cocktail" as the ultimate panacea, a remedy for all of life's problems, whether it's a hangover, a case of the Mondays, or a stubbed toe. Their commitment to the Bloody Mary is so profound that they might even claim it can cure existential crises or bring about world peace, one celery stick at a time. And yes, they firmly believe that drinking another Bloody Mary is the surefire way to cure the hangover from the previous ones, creating a never-ending cycle of tomato-induced recovery. Watch as they carefully assemble their salad skewers, turning the drink into a well-balanced meal. As they sip, they appear to be invincible, or so they would like to believe.

Long Island Iced Tea Lovers

Ahoy there, matey! These swashbuckling aficionados of Long Island Iced Tea are convinced that sipping on this boozy blend of spirits is like embarking on a high-seas adventure. With each tall glass, they are setting sail on a voyage on to an island paradise, even if that island is just their neighbor's pool deck. Watch as they passionately list off the ingredients like a ship's captain reciting a treasure map, proclaiming, "Rum, vodka, gin, and tequila? Aye, we've hit the jackpot!" They're the kind of folks who garnish their drinks with tiny paper umbrellas, mini surfboards, and plastic flamingos, turning any gathering into a tropical luau, or at least a tropical-themed garage party. With their infectious enthusiasm, you might find yourself yearning for a straw hat and a penchant for exaggerated pirate accents by the time you finish your Long Island Iced Tea. Arrr, matey!

White Wine Aficionados

These enthusiasts of white wine are as serene as a cat's nap in a sunbeam, sipping their crisp Chardonnays and Sauvignon Blancs as if they were gracefully tiptoeing through a sun-kissed vineyard. They approach their wine with the elegance of a swan gliding across a pristine lake, always aiming for a light and airy experience. You will often find them in the wine aisle, choosing bottles based on the whimsical shape of the label or how well the wine complements their summer wardrobe. For them, a glass of white wine is like a gentle zephyr on a warm day, capable of soothing their souls and transporting them to a mental picnic under a tree adorned with cheese and crackers.

Red Wine Enthusiasts

These passionate red wine aficionados are the consummate storytellers of the beverage world. They approach their glasses of Cabernets and Merlots with the kind of reverence one might reserve for a rare, ancient tome, swirling and sniffing as if they were unearthing the secrets of a lost civilization. To them, each sip is like turning a page in a classic novel—rich, complex, and filled with character. You might catch them at wine tastings, sharing elaborate narratives about the history of each vineyard, complete with dramatic plot twists involving soil composition and grape varietals. Their penchant for swirling can rival a professional cyclone chaser, and their descriptions of wine notes could put even the most verbose poet to shame. For these enthusiasts, wine is not just a beverage; it is a literary journey, and they are the Hemingways and Austens of the wine-tasting world, with an uncanny ability to make you believe that a glass of red wine contains the secrets of the universe.

Mimosa Mavens

These dedicated mimosa lovers are the perpetual brunch-goers who have mastered the art of turning every morning into a celebration. With their bubbly concoction of champagne and orange juice, they possess the unique ability to transform even the dreariest of weekdays into a Sunday brunch party.

They treat every sunrise like a grand event, complete with confetti cannons and a marching band. You will find them in their element at brunch spots, where they clink glasses with enthusiasm that rivals a touchdown celebration at the Super Bowl. For Mimosa Mavens, life is a perpetual brunch, and they believe that orange juice is the elixir of vitality, while champagne is the nectar of the gods.

Expect them to suggest mimosas for breakfast meetings, job interviews, and even during interstellar travel—they firmly believe that mimosas are the universal language of happiness.

Cognac Connoisseurs

These refined aficionados of the world's finest brandy, Cognac, carry themselves with the air of aristocrats from a bygone era. Each sip of Cognac is, to them, a transcendental journey to a grand chateau nestled in the heart of the French countryside, complete with sweeping vineyards and tapestries that whisper tales of centuries past. They approach their glass with the solemnity of a sommelier presenting a rare vintage, swirling it delicately to awaken its intricate bouquet of aromas, as if coaxing secrets from an ancient tome. Cognac Connoisseurs are walking encyclopedias of fine spirits, regaling anyone within earshot with tales of Cognac's history, from the rolling hills of the Charente region to the distillation process that turns humble grapes into liquid gold. They revere the amber liquid as if it were a work of art, ascribing poetic descriptions to the notes of dried fruits, oak, and subtle spices that dance on their palates. To them, Cognac is more than a drink; it's an embodiment of elegance and sophistication. They may speak of "V.S.O.P" and "X.O" with the reverence others reserve for secret society codes, and they appreciate the finest crystal glassware as a vessel to elevate the Cognac experience. In their presence, you might find yourself unintentionally adjusting your posture, speaking more eloquently, and contemplating the finer aspects of life, all while being transported to the hallowed halls of French nobility with every sip. It is as if they have unlocked the door to a timeless realm where Cognac is the elixir of sophistication itself.

17

THE DILEMMA

"**I**'m miserable," grumbled one flat flea to its companion, nestled snugly in the Yarkand hare's straight, sandy brown dorsal fur, ready to feed.

"We're living the life. You're too negative," retorted the other flea.

"Is this what you call life?" sighed the discontented flea.

"Why are you dissatisfied?" questioned its companion.

"Oh, where do I begin? The living conditions are dreadful, and the blood tastes like grass. Yuk!"

"We have food, shelter, and warmth," insisted the content flea.

Silence lingered as the flat flea pondered these responses. It glanced around, trying to see what its companion saw—food, shelter, and warmth. Yet the flat flea remained unsatisfied; it yearned for more.

"You're complacent. That's your problem. It's dangerous, you know," the discontented flea continued, its rant culminating in a bold suggestion. "We should find another host."

"Why?" queried the other flea.

"For better circumstances, if we seek only food, shelter, and warmth, we can find them elsewhere," argued the discontented flea.

"Our circumstances are adequate, but I understand your point," conceded the content flea.

"It will be an improvement. Follow me," urged the flea, and together they leaped onto a nearby rat.

The rat scurried faster than the hare, yet the ride was smoother and less bumpy. "Woo-hoo!" exclaimed the flea, expressing its thrill. It would have tipped its hat, imagining itself like a rodeo rider atop a bronco.

The rat's tiny claws whispered against the wheat field, then clanked loudly on the city's cobblestone roads, eventually crossing a wooden plank. Finally, it halted, its pink nose twitching in the air, sniffing the salty sea mixed with the scent of grain it pursued.

The fleas feasted to delirium on their new host, only to find the rat stiff and still when hunger called again. Poison had ended its life. Hungry, cold, and desperate, the fleas embarked on the search for their next meal and shelter—not the rosy picture painted by the discontented flea while nestled in the hare's fur.

Wary of the dangers lurking in the ship's hold—abundant grain but also lethal poison—the fleas hesitated. In dire times, drastic measures were necessary, and soon they struck fortune. A man entered the musty darkness, filling his pitcher with rum from the barrels. The fleas seized their chance.

The rum was sweet, spicy, and spiked—a perfect blend. The oriental flat fleas spent their flea lives breeding and feeding on sailors as the ship sailed across the Mediterranean from Constantinople to Sicily in the summer of 1347, carrying more than just dreams and merchandise in its hold.

18

ZODIACS

Fasten your cosmic seatbelts, because we're about to take a hilarious tour through the zodiac! Here are the zaniest, quirkiest, and downright silliest descriptions of your star signs that the universe has ever seen. So, hold on to your horoscopes, because things are about to get astrologically absurd.

Aries (March 21–April 19):

Aries are the cosmic wildfire of the zodiac. You blaze through life with the intensity of a bull in a china shop after downing several energy drinks. Your entrance into any room is akin to a thunderstorm—sudden, electrifying, and impossible to ignore. Each day, you transform mundane moments into accidental performance art pieces, leaving a trail of astonished and amused onlookers in your wake.

Patience? That's just an eight-letter word you don't have time for. You're the embodiment of impulsiveness, preferring to speed headfirst into challenges rather than wait for the door to open.

Every challenge in your life presents an opportunity for a spectacular crash and an immediate, fearless recovery, much like a never-ending game of demolition derby.

Yet, amidst the chaos you create, there's a magnetic charm that draws people to you. Your unpredictability keeps us on our toes, constantly guessing what your next move will be. While your path might seem chaotic, there's a method to your madness—a relentless drive that fuels your journey. Your determination is as steadfast as a dog chasing its own tail, undeterred by the dizzying pursuit. It's this fierce persistence that transforms your hilarious mishaps into legendary tales of resilience and adventure.

In a world that often treads too carefully, you're a breath of fresh air—a whirlwind of energy and enthusiasm that reminds us that life is meant to be lived boldly, with a fearless heart and a fiery spirit. Your presence is a testament to the power of embracing one's true nature, no matter how wild or unpredictable it may be.

Taurus (April 20–May 20):

Taurus, you're the living, breathing embodiment of the motto, "If it ain't broke, don't fix it." Your steadfastness could make a mule blush and say, "Take a chill pill, dude."

While the rest of us ride life's roller-coaster, speed dating experiences like they're Tinder profiles, you prefer to lounge in the corner, savoring life's buffet as if it were a five-course feast. You find joy in the slow, deliberate moments where every bite, sip, and sensation is a celebration of existence.

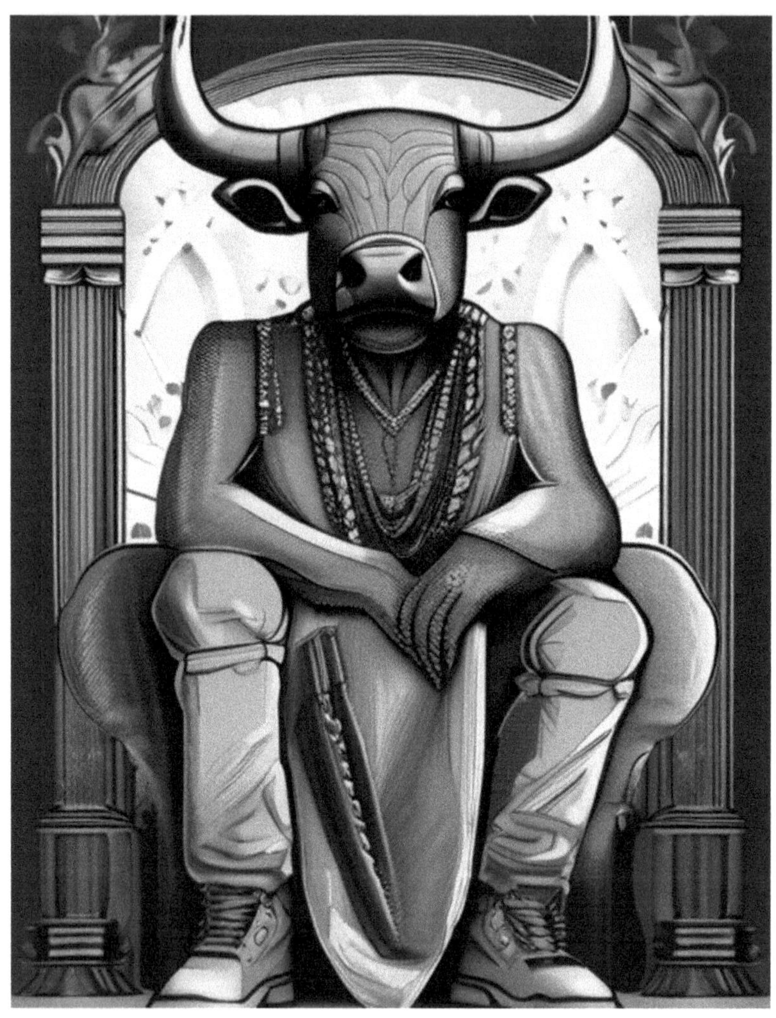

Your loyalty is unwavering, a rock in the often turbulent sea of life. Friends and loved ones can always count on you to be their anchor, offering stability and a sense of calm amidst the chaos. Your love for the finer things in life transforms you into the unapologetic hedonist of the zodiac. You don't just smell the roses;

you cultivate entire botanical gardens, tending to each bloom with meticulous care and unhurried grace.

In a world obsessed with speed and novelty, you're a connoisseur of tradition and comfort. Whether it's a well-worn leather chair, a vintage wine, or a perfectly cooked meal, you appreciate the craftsmanship and history behind every cherished possession and experience. Your home is a sanctuary, filled with plush textures, rich scents, and a sense of timeless elegance that invites everyone to relax and stay awhile.

While your stubbornness can be a double-edged sword, leading to occasional clashes with those who prefer a more spontaneous approach, it's also the bedrock of your character. This trait ensures that once you set your mind on something—or someone—you're all in, committed for the long haul. You move through life at a deliberate pace, savoring each moment and leaving a trail of beauty and stability wherever you go.

Your presence is a reminder that life's true pleasures are found in consistency, loyalty, and the sensory richness of the world around us. You teach us the value of patience and the joy of indulging in life's simple yet profound luxuries, one deliberate moment at a time.

Gemini (May 21–June 20):

Geminis, you're the cosmic plate-spinners of the zodiac. You possess more personalities than a Netflix series has plot twists. Keeping up with your mood swings is like chasing a hyperactive squirrel through a maze of emotions, each turn revealing a new and unexpected facet of your character. One moment, you're the life of the party, dazzling everyone with your quick wit and infectious energy;

the next, you're a deep thinker, lost in a philosophical reverie that leaves us all wondering what profound insight you'll share next.

Navigating life with a Gemini is akin to using a GPS on a caffeine overdose. If you ever find yourself lost, just ask a Gemini for directions—they'll provide you with a menu of choices, each path leading in a different direction, leaving you both amused and slightly bewildered. Your mind is a whirlwind of ideas, constantly generating new possibilities and perspectives. This boundless curiosity makes you an engaging conversationalist, capable of turning any mundane topic into a lively debate or a fascinating discussion.

Your dual nature can be both a blessing and a challenge for those around you. On one hand, your adaptability and resourcefulness mean you can thrive in almost any situation, effortlessly switching gears and taking on new roles with ease. On the other hand, your unpredictability can be a rollercoaster for those who prefer stability, as they never quite know which version of you they'll encounter next.

But it's this very unpredictability that keeps us entertained and drawn to you. Your witty charm is irresistible, your stories captivating, and your insights often unexpectedly profound. You bring a sense of excitement and spontaneity to every interaction, turning conversations into dynamic games of cosmic ping-pong. Each exchange with you is an adventure, full of twists and turns that leave us both breathless and exhilarated.

In a world that often craves predictability and routine, you're a breath of fresh air, reminding us of the beauty of change and the thrill of discovery. Your multifaceted personality and insatiable curiosity inspire us to embrace the unknown and find joy in the endless variety of life's experiences. Whether you're dazzling us with your charm or challenging us with your intellect, you're the vibrant spark that lights up our lives, a true Gemini in all your complex, captivating glory.

Cancer (June 21–July 22):

Cancer, you're the zodiac's resident tear fountain, embodying the emotional heartbeat of the astrological wheel. With your heart worn boldly on your sleeve like a trendy new accessory, you navigate the world with a raw openness that is both disarming and endearing.

Your emotions are displayed as vividly as a billboard in Times Square, leaving no doubt about what you're feeling at any given moment.

One moment, you're the nurturing mother hen, gathering your loved ones under your protective wing and offering comfort and care with unmatched tenderness. You have an innate ability to sense when someone is in need, and your compassionate nature compels you to be their emotional anchor. However, this sensitivity can also be your Achilles' heel. The slightest disturbance—a harsh word, a disapproving glance, or even a sneeze in your general direction—can send you retreating into a protective shell, curled up in a fetal position, seeking solace from the world's harshness.

Your empathy and emotional depth run deeper than a mole in a tunneling competition, making you the friend we all secretly need in our lives. Your capacity for understanding and sharing the feelings of others is profound, allowing you to connect on a level that few others can. You have an uncanny ability to offer comfort and guidance, often knowing just the right words to say to heal a wounded heart or to provide reassurance in times of doubt.

However, your presence at social gatherings can sometimes turn them into live soap operas. Your heightened emotional awareness and expressive nature mean that every event is rich with drama and intensity. While this can be overwhelming for some, it also adds a layer of depth and authenticity to interactions, turning ordinary moments into memorable experiences.

In a world that often prizes emotional restraint and stoicism, you remind us of the power and beauty of vulnerability. Your willingness to feel deeply and to express those feelings openly is a testament to your strength. You teach us that it is okay to be in touch with our emotions, to cry when we're hurt, and to love fiercely and unconditionally.

Your ability to transform ordinary life into a tapestry of rich, emotional experiences makes you an invaluable friend and confidant. With you, we learn the importance of empathy, the healing power of a heartfelt hug, and the strength found in true emotional connection. You're the comforting presence in a stormy sea, a reminder that amidst the chaos of life, there's always room for love and understanding.

Leo (July 23–August 22):

Leos are the monarchs of the astro-jungle. You reign supreme with a confidence so unshakable that it could make the sun itself second-guess its position at the center of the universe. Your conviction that the cosmos revolves around you is so strong that even the planets seem to send you fan mail, acknowledging your celestial charisma. Attention is your lifeblood, more essential than a cat's obsessive desire to knock over a tower of empty boxes. You bask in the spotlight with the fervor of a toddler having a tantrum in a toy store, yet, unlike the toddler, you're the toy everyone eagerly wants to engage with, drawn to your magnetic allure.

Your larger-than-life personality is an extravagant spectacle, turning every mundane moment into a grand performance. Whether it's your infectious laughter, your dramatic flair, or your undeniable charm, you captivate those around you, making sure that all eyes are firmly fixed on you. Your presence commands attention, and you thrive on the adoration and admiration that follow you wherever you go.

But beneath that glittering exterior lies a heart as precious as a glittery doughnut—sweet, delightful, and filled with warmth. Your loyalty to those you consider your pride is unwavering, mirroring a penguin's steadfast commitment to its tuxedo collection. You cherish your loved ones with a fierceness that rivals your own need for adulation, always ready to protect and support them with regal devotion.

Your loyalty is not just an act; it is a deeply ingrained part of who you are. You stand by your friends and family through thick and thin, offering a shoulder to lean on and a courageous spirit to rally around. Your generosity knows no bounds, as you give of yourself selflessly, ensuring that those you care about feel valued and cherished.

In social gatherings, your presence is like a burst of sunshine, illuminating the room and lifting everyone's spirits. Your natural leadership qualities often put you at the forefront, guiding others with a sense of purpose and direction. You inspire confidence and courage in those around you, encouraging them to embrace their own inner strengths and shine brightly.

Yet, it's not just your flamboyance that makes you special; it's your ability to make others feel seen and appreciated. You have a knack for recognizing the unique qualities in everyone, celebrating their individuality, and making them feel like stars in your grand constellation. This rare gift of uplifting others while dazzling them with your own brilliance is what sets you apart as the true monarch of the zodiac jungle.

In a world that often dims its lights, you, Leo, remind us to embrace our full selves, to stand tall, and to never shy away from the spotlight. You teach us the importance of confidence, loyalty, and the joy of living life with unabashed enthusiasm. With you, we learn that life is not just to be lived but to be celebrated with all the pomp and grandeur it deserves.

Virgo (August 23–September 22):

Virgos, you're the ultimate cosmic nitpickers, masters of meticulous detail and precision. Your attention to the smallest elements is so sharp that even Sherlock Holmes would need a magnifying glass to keep up with your to-do lists. You dissect tasks with an analytical mind, leaving no stone unturned and no item unchecked. Your ability to notice and address the minutiae is unparalleled, making you the go-to person for solving complex problems and uncovering hidden truths.

Your obsession with cleanliness and organization is legendary. So intense is your need for order that Marie Kondo herself would probably seek your advice on decluttering. You have an uncanny talent for transforming chaos into serene, structured environments. Your surroundings reflect your inner world—neat, orderly, and impeccably organized. You approach each task with a methodical precision that is nothing short of awe-inspiring. Your living space is a testament to your organizational prowess, where even the most mundane items find their perfect place, neatly arranged and easily accessible.

In your world, everything has a purpose and a designated spot. Your closet is not just a place to store clothes; it is a marvel of precision, with items categorized, color-coded, and filed in a system so efficient it could rival the best filing cabinets. Your sock drawer is a work of art, each pair neatly folded and aligned with military precision. The sight of such order is both impressive and envy-inducing, leaving others wondering how you manage to maintain such impeccable standards.

However, your quest for perfection does come with a price. The only thing you sacrifice for all that order is spontaneity. You prefer structure and predictability over the unexpected. Your love for planning and preparation means you rarely leave things to chance. Spontaneity is not a concept that fits neatly into your well-ordered life. But who needs it when your sock drawer is a marvel of precision and your daily routines run like clockwork?

Your meticulous nature extends beyond physical spaces to every aspect of your life. You're detail-oriented in your work, relationships, and even in your leisure activities. You have a knack for spotting inconsistencies and improving systems, making you an invaluable asset to any team or project. Your friends and family appreciate your reliability and the sense of calm you bring with your organized approach.

Yet, beneath the surface of your perfectionist exterior lies a heart that genuinely cares. Your meticulous attention to detail is driven by a desire to make the world a better place, one well-organized space at a time. You derive satisfaction from helping others find clarity and order in their lives, offering practical solutions and thoughtful advice. Your dedication to improving your surroundings and the lives of those around you is a testament to your selfless nature.

In a world that often values speed and superficiality, you, Virgo, remind us of the importance of thoroughness and care. You teach us that true excellence lies in the details and that order and beauty can coexist harmoniously. Your presence is a calming influence, inspiring us to strive for our best and appreciate the serenity that comes with a well-organized life. With you, we learn that a little bit of precision can go a long way in creating a harmonious and fulfilling existence.

Libra (September 23–October 22):

Libras are the zodiac's never-ending peacemakers. You embody the essence of harmony and balance in a world often fraught with conflict. You would rather bite your tongue than engage in a verbal joust, avoiding confrontation with a finesse that borders on the extraordinary. Your pursuit of equilibrium is like trying to balance a cat on a unicycle—precarious, delicate, and requiring immense skill. Yet, you approach this challenge with a calm demeanor and an unwavering dedication to maintaining peace.

You're the human equivalent of a seesaw caught in an earthquake, oscillating wildly in your quest for balance. Every decision is weighed meticulously, every outcome considered, as you strive to create an environment where everyone feels valued and understood. This constant balancing act can be exhausting, but your commitment to fairness and justice keeps you steadfast. You seek to find the middle ground in every situation, ensuring that all perspectives are acknowledged and respected.

Despite the internal turmoil that this quest for harmony can sometimes cause, your outward persona is a beacon of charm and grace. You have an innate ability to make everyone around you feel special and appreciated, like they've just won a lifetime supply of chocolate-covered donuts. Your social skills are second to none, effortlessly navigating conversations and social settings with a blend of tact, wit, and genuine interest in others. Your presence has a soothing effect, turning anger and resentment into fleeting memories faster than you can say, "Mind your manners."

Your charm isn't just surface-level; it's deeply rooted in your genuine desire to see people happy and at peace. You possess a unique ability to diffuse tension and foster understanding, making you a beloved friend and confidant. Your diplomatic skills are legendary, and your advice is often sought in times of discord. You have a talent for seeing all sides of a situation, offering balanced and thoughtful perspectives that help others find common ground.

However, this relentless pursuit of harmony can sometimes lead to indecision as you weigh every option in search of the perfect solution. You may find yourself caught in a perpetual loop of "what ifs," hesitant to take definitive action for fear of upsetting the delicate balance you strive to maintain. But this caution is also a testament to your deep sense of responsibility and your commitment to making choices that benefit everyone involved.

Your love for beauty and aesthetics extends beyond your social interactions. You have an eye for design and a penchant for creating environments that are both beautiful and inviting. Whether it's your home, your wardrobe, or the way you present yourself, everything you touch is imbued with a sense of elegance and style. This appreciation for beauty is not just about appearances; it is about creating spaces and experiences that uplift and inspire.

In a world that often prioritizes winning over understanding, you, Libra, are a reminder of the power of empathy and the importance of seeing the bigger picture. You teach us that true strength lies in the ability to foster connection and that peace is worth pursuing, even when the path is fraught with challenges. Your grace, charm, and unwavering commitment to harmony make you a guiding light, showing us the way to a more balanced and compassionate world.

Scorpio (October 23–November 21):

Scorpios are the resident secret agents of the zodiac. You cloak your emotions with the precision and secrecy of the FBI, leaving those around you perpetually intrigued and slightly mystified.

Your inner world is a labyrinth of deep feelings and profound thoughts, guarded fiercely against any unwanted intrusion. To truly know a Scorpio is to embark on a journey filled with twists and turns, akin to navigating the plot of a gripping Netflix thriller.

Your idea of a romantic date is anything but conventional. Where others might opt for a candlelit dinner or a walk on the beach, you gravitate towards the extraordinary and the enigmatic. A midnight séance in a haunted house, complete with flickering candles and whispered secrets, is far more your speed. You thrive in the shadows, drawn to the mysterious and the unknown, and you seek out experiences that mirror the intensity of your own emotions.

Your intensity is palpable, radiating an energy that can be both magnetic and intimidating. People are drawn to your enigmatic aura, sensing that beneath your calm exterior lies a well of unspoken passion and unyielding determination. Your presence alone can command a room, and your gaze, often described as piercing, seems to see right through to the core of a person's soul.

Yet, despite the occasional eerie vibe you might give off, your loyalty and passion are unshakeable. When you commit to someone or something, you do so with a depth that is rarely matched. Your loyalty is as steadfast as it is intense, and those fortunate enough to earn it know they have an ally who will stand by them through thick and thin. Your dedication is unwavering, and you approach relationships with the same fervor and intensity that you bring to all aspects of your life.

However, your intensity and secretive nature can sometimes creep people out more than a surprise clown at a birthday party. Your tendency to withhold your emotions and thoughts can create an air of mystery that, while intriguing, can also be unsettling to those who prefer transparency and openness. But this is simply part of the Scorpio charm—a complex mix of allure and enigma that keeps others guessing and captivated.

Under the layers of mystery and intensity lies a heart capable of profound love and deep connections. Your relationships, though sometimes challenging due to your passionate nature, are marked by a level of intimacy and loyalty that is unparalleled. You have an innate ability to connect with others on a soul-deep level, understanding their deepest fears and desires without them uttering a single word.

In a world that often values superficial connections and fleeting encounters, you, Scorpio, remind us of the power and beauty of deep, unspoken bonds. Your presence challenges us to look beyond the surface and to embrace the complexities of our own emotions. You teach us that true connection requires vulnerability and trust, and that the most meaningful relationships are built on a foundation of unyielding loyalty and passion.

Your life is a testament to the strength and resilience of the human spirit. You face challenges head-on, unafraid of the darkness, and you emerge stronger and more determined each time. With your unwavering intensity and profound loyalty, you show us that true strength lies in embracing our deepest selves and in forging connections that transcend the ordinary.

Sagittarius (November 22–December 21):

Sagittarians are the eternal wanderlusters of the zodiac. You're driven by an insatiable desire to explore and experience the world. Staying in one place for too long feels like a prison sentence, and the mere thought of a routine makes you more elusive than a ninja's cat on roller skates. Your spirit yearns for adventure, and you're always ready to jet-set with flamingos in a Hawaiian shirt, embracing the thrill of the unknown and the excitement of new horizons.

Commitment to a routine? That's a concept that's as foreign to you as winter is to the tropics. You shun the mundane and the predictable, preferring instead to follow the call of the wild and the allure of distant lands. Your life is a never-ending quest for novelty and excitement, where each day is an opportunity to discover something new and extraordinary. You're the epitome of a free spirit, untethered and unbound by the constraints that hold others back.

While the rest of us are busy adulting and doing our taxes, you're out there globe-trotting like a ninja clown on a pogo stick, bouncing from one adventure to the next with boundless energy and enthusiasm. Responsibilities? You treat them like pesky mosquitoes at a BBQ—easily ignored and swiftly swatted away. Your phone is often left unanswered as you immerse yourself in the vibrant mosaic of life, preferring the immediacy of real-world experiences over the demands of modern communication.

Your wanderlust isn't just about physical travel; it's a reflection of your inner quest for knowledge and wisdom. You have a deep-seated curiosity about the world and a burning desire to understand different cultures, philosophies, and perspectives. This intellectual hunger drives you to explore not just places, but ideas and beliefs, making you a perpetual student of life. Your open-mindedness and love for learning are infectious, inspiring those around you to broaden their own horizons and seek out new experiences.

Despite your seemingly carefree attitude, there's a profound depth to your explorations. You're not just a tourist; you're a true traveler, seeking to connect with the soul of each place you visit and the people you meet. Your journeys are filled with meaningful encounters and transformative experiences that shape your worldview and enrich your understanding of humanity.

In relationships, your free-spirited nature can be both exhilarating and challenging. You bring a sense of adventure and spontaneity that keeps things exciting, but your reluctance to be tied down can sometimes leave your partner's feeling unsteady. Yet, those who understand and appreciate your need for freedom find in you a passionate and devoted companion, someone who brings joy, excitement, and a refreshing perspective to life.

Your optimism and zest for life are contagious. You approach each day with a sense of wonder and possibility, believing that the world is full of opportunities waiting to be discovered. Your positivity and enthusiasm light up any room, turning ordinary moments into extraordinary memories.

In a world that often emphasizes stability and routine, you, Sagittarius, remind us of the beauty of exploration and the importance of following our dreams. You teach us that life is an adventure meant to be lived to the fullest, and that true happiness comes from embracing the unknown and taking bold steps into the future. Your boundless energy and unwavering spirit of adventure make you a beacon of inspiration, encouraging us all to break free from our comfort zones and embark on our own journeys of discovery.

Capricorn (December 22–January 19):

Capricorns are the zodiac's fearless workaholics. You're the embodiment of ambition and relentless determination. You approach your goals with a precision and focus that puts the "pro" in procrastination, turning what might seem like mundane tasks into extraordinary feats of productivity. While others are unwinding on a Friday night, you're deep into your latest project, transforming your workspace into an Excel spreadsheet pajama party, where formulas and data cells dance with organized enthusiasm.

Your ability to manage your time and responsibilities is nothing short of legendary. While the rest of us are frantically searching for matching socks in the morning chaos, you're already knee-deep in tackling spreadsheets, wielding your calculator with the expertise of a ninja accountant. Projects that might overwhelm others are your playgrounds, and you handle them with the grace and agility of a squirrel on a caffeine high. Your work ethic is unrivaled, and your ability to juggle multiple tasks with ease is a testament to your incredible organizational skills and disciplined approach.

We secretly admire your ambition and determination, often in awe of how seamlessly you transition from one task to another, all while maintaining a level of professionalism and dedication that seems superhuman. Your ability to "adult" like a pro, managing responsibilities, deadlines, and personal goals with finesse, is something we aspire to. While we stumble through adulthood like amateurs at a dessert buffet, overwhelmed by choices and distractions, you navigate it with clarity and purpose, always keeping your eyes on the prize.

Yet, beneath your serious and disciplined exterior lies a heart that deeply cares about the people and goals you invest in. Your loyalty and commitment extend beyond your work, as you bring the same level of dedication to your relationships and personal endeavors. You are the rock that others lean on, providing stability and support in times of need. Your practical advice and grounded perspective are invaluable, helping those around you to stay focused and achieve their own aspirations.

Your sense of responsibility is matched by a quiet but unwavering determination. You're not one to seek the spotlight, preferring to let your hard work and accomplishments speak for themselves. Your perseverance is a beacon of inspiration, showing us all that success is achieved through consistent effort and a steadfast commitment to one's goals.

In social settings, your presence brings a sense of calm and order. While you may not be the life of the party, your dry wit and subtle humor often leave a lasting impression. You have a knack for making others feel at ease, offering practical solutions and sage advice that cut through the noise and get to the heart of the matter. Your wisdom and reliability make you a cherished friend and confidant.

In a world that often prioritizes instant gratification and shortcuts, you, Capricorn, remind us of the value of hard work, patience, and perseverance. You teach us that true success is built on a foundation of dedication and discipline and that the rewards of our efforts are well worth the time and energy invested. Your relentless pursuit of excellence and your unwavering commitment to your goals make you a guiding light, encouraging us all to strive for our best and to embrace the journey with the same fearless determination that you embody every day.

Aquarius (January 20–February 18):

Aquarians are the cosmic dreamers of the zodiac. You're the visionary pioneers charting unknown territories in the vast expanse of imagination. Your mind is like a laboratory of innovative ideas, where mad science and creativity blend seamlessly. You wear your eccentricity proudly, like a badge of honor, embodying the essence of a mad scientist who has accidentally spilled daydream potions all over their lab coat. While the rest of us are stuck in the mundane reality of the present, struggling like folks trying to find a Wi-Fi signal in the '90s, you're already light years ahead, attending alien conventions and discussing conspiracy theories with an enthusiasm that could rival a squirrel on an espresso binge.

Your intellect is a dazzling array of unconventional thoughts and revolutionary ideas. You perceive the world through a kaleidoscope of possibilities, seeing potential and wonder where others see only routine and predictability. Conversations with you're like embarking on a journey through a galaxy of curiosity and discovery. You effortlessly dive into topics that range from the bizarre to the profound, leaving us both baffled and intrigued by your Rubik's cube of quirkiness.

Your eccentricity is not just for show; it is a core part of your identity that fuels your relentless pursuit of knowledge and understanding. You're a natural-born innovator, constantly questioning the status quo and pushing the boundaries of what's possible. Whether you're exploring the mysteries of the universe, advocating for social change, or simply daydreaming about futuristic worlds, your thoughts and actions are driven by a deep desire to make the world a better place.

In social settings, your presence is magnetic. People are drawn to your unique perspective and charismatic energy. You have an uncanny ability to make even the most mundane topics fascinating, weaving your web of ideas with the skill of a master storyteller. Your enthusiasm is infectious, inspiring those around you to look beyond their immediate surroundings and consider the bigger picture.

While your eccentricity can sometimes leave others scratching their heads, it also serves as a reminder of the beauty of diversity and individuality. You challenge us to embrace our own quirks and to think outside the box, encouraging a sense of freedom and creativity that's often suppressed in our daily lives. Your unconventional approach to life is a breath of fresh air, shaking us out of our complacency and reminding us that there is so much more to explore and discover.

Your dedication to your ideals and causes is unwavering. You're a champion of progress and innovation, often leading the charge in efforts to create positive change in the world. Your humanitarian spirit is evident in your actions and your unwavering commitment to making a difference. You're not content with simply dreaming of a better future; you actively work towards creating it, inspiring others to join you on this noble quest.

In a world that often values conformity and tradition, you, Aquarius, are a beacon of originality and forward-thinking. You teach us that true progress is achieved by daring to dream and by embracing the unknown with open arms. Your visionary mindset and boundless curiosity remind us that the future is full of possibilities waiting to be explored. With you, we learn to embrace our inner dreamers and to never stop questioning, innovating, and striving for a better tomorrow.

Pisces (February 19–March 20):

Pisces. The dreamy escape artists of the zodiac. You glide through life with an ethereal grace that defies the constraints of reality. You're the human equivalent of a daydream on roller skates, effortlessly floating through experiences like a ping-pong ball in a tornado, unpredictable yet captivating. For you, reality is a distant concept, as elusive as trying to teach a giraffe to moonwalk—just not happening. Your world is one of fantasy and imagination, where the lines between dreams and reality blur into a beautiful mosaic of possibilities.

Your emotions ebb and flow with a rhythm that's uniquely your own, more unpredictable than a squirrel on a pogo stick. One moment, you're riding a wave of joy, lost in the beauty of a sunset or the melody of a favorite song; the next, you might be swept away by a current of melancholy, feeling the weight of the world's sorrows. This emotional fluidity is both your strength and your challenge, allowing you to connect deeply with others but also making it difficult for you to anchor yourself in the mundane.

It wouldn't surprise anyone who knows you if you secretly believed you could have heart-to-heart chats with dolphins. Your empathy and intuition are so finely tuned that you often seem to communicate on a wavelength that transcends the ordinary. You have an uncanny ability to sense what others are feeling, offering comfort and understanding with a kindness that is almost magical. This deep emotional intelligence makes you a cherished friend and confidant, someone who can turn even the most ordinary moments into whimsical adventures.

Your creativity is like a magic wand, transforming everyday experiences into something extraordinary. Whether you're crafting a piece of art, writing a poem, or simply telling a story, you bring a touch of enchantment to everything you do. Your imaginative spirit inspires those around you, encouraging them to see the world through a lens of wonder and possibility. You have a gift for finding beauty in the mundane and for making the ordinary seem extraordinary.

In social settings, your dreamy nature is both intriguing and comforting. People are drawn to your gentle aura and your ability to make them feel seen and understood. You have a way of making everyone feel special, weaving them into your world of dreams and fantasies with a genuine warmth that is hard to resist. Your conversations are like stepping into a fairy tale, where anything is possible and reality is just a stepping stone to greater adventures.

While your penchant for escapism can sometimes make it challenging to deal with practical matters, it also allows you to navigate life's difficulties with a resilience born of imagination. You find solace in your dreams and creative pursuits, using them as a sanctuary from the harshness of the real world. This ability to retreat into your inner world helps you maintain your balance and find joy even in challenging times.

In a world that often demands conformity and practicality, you, Pisces, are a reminder of the power of dreams and the importance of staying connected to our inner child. You teach us that there is magic to be found in the everyday and that our imaginations can be a source of strength and inspiration. Your whimsical spirit and boundless empathy make you a beacon of hope and creativity, encouraging us all to embrace our dreams and see the world through your enchanted eyes. With you, we learn that life is not just about surviving but about finding the magic and wonder that make it truly worth living.

19

THE FIRST MURDER

The sun descended behind the distant horizon, casting fiery red hues across the sky. The sweltering heat still clung to the barren landscape as distant murmurs from the nearby town drifted through the air. On the outskirts, two enigmatic figures, Simon and John, stood together, their silhouettes barely distinguishable against the dimming light. They huddled over a grim pool of blood, shrouded in an eerie atmosphere.

"This scene gives me the creeps, John. What kind of twisted individual could commit such an act?" Simon inquired, adjusting his gloves nervously.

"Whoever it was, they must have acted out of anger. Just look at the devastation they've caused," John responded, narrowing his eyes at the chilling bloodstains on the ground.

Crime scene technicians kneeled with care, meticulously scrutinizing the area around the lifeless body. Simon reached into his kit, pulling out an evidence bag with precision.

The victim, a young man in his early twenties, lay partially dressed, bearing a ghastly head wound. As darkness gradually enveloped the scene, John passed a light to Simon.

"Be careful, Simon. We must collect every piece of evidence without risking contamination," John warned, his voice laden with gravitas.

Simon nodded solemnly, gripping the light with steady hands. He positioned it over the gruesome scene, scanning carefully for valuable clues. A blood-splattered rock caught Simon's eye, prompting him to approach for a closer inspection.

"Hey John," Simon called out, "I believe I've found something."

"It certainly appears to be a potential murder weapon," John agreed cautiously, emphasizing the need for a detective's final determination. Simon gingerly placed the bloodied rock into the bag.

With precision and diligence, the two technicians gathered an assortment of evidence, meticulously labeling each item, ensuring nothing was overlooked in their quest for justice.

The grim tidings of a murder quickly coursed through the village, prompting a gradual gathering of onlookers. Simon and John exchanged exasperated glances, silently hoping to fulfill their duties without an intrusive crowd observing their every move. However, their wishes were in vain, for the villagers had already converged upon the scene, their footsteps disturbing the tranquility as they trod over rocks and bushes, jostling for a better view.

"Ugh," Simon grumbled, attempting to drown out the murmurings of the assembled crowd.

"Perhaps someone among them can help identify the victim," John optimistically suggested, striving to find a silver lining in the crowd that surrounded them.

"It won't be easy. The poor soul's countenance is beyond recognition," Simon concluded with a heavy sigh, gently turning the lifeless body.

The gruesome scene enthralled the onlookers. Distressed women wept and shielded the eyes of their children, sparing them from the harrowing sight. A herd of sheep leisurely made their way towards the group as they aimlessly foraged for sustenance in the desolate terrain, paying little heed to the crowd.

"Someone ought to lead this herd of sheep away," Simon muttered, frustration evident in his voice. The chaotic juxtaposition of life and death only added to the overwhelming sense of despair that hung in the air.

John stood up and scanned his surroundings. "I wonder who owns these sheep. I don't see the shepherd anywhere."

The crowd grew increasingly anxious over the presence of the unattended sheep, their unease magnified by the eerie silence that enveloped the desolate terrain. Whispers of concern and speculation rippled through the onlookers, intensifying their collective urgency to locate the sheep's owner, effectively diverting their attention from the grim scene and the lifeless body.

Darkness blanketed the landscape, casting long shadows that seemed to dance with the flickering flames of nearby torches. The absence of any sign of life, coupled with the chilling silence, deepened the sense of foreboding that gripped everyone present. It was as if the sheep and their mysterious appearance were harbingers of something far more sinister lurking in the shadows.

Far off in the distance, a tiny glimmer of light materialized, steadily approaching. As it drew near, the faint shuffle of footsteps against the ground gradually became more distinct, resonating through the hushed atmosphere. The suspense thickened as the figure materialized from the darkness, their resolute expression coming into view. A young man moved forward, his gaze sweeping across the assembled faces, just as a woman urgently made her way through the crowd.

"Where's your brother?"

The man looked around nervously, his eyes darting from person to person. Sweat began to bead on his forehead as he hesitated, unsure of how to respond.

Simon held the light up to the young man and noticed blood on his hands. Simon's heart raced, and his mind flooded with questions. He grabbed John's arm, who quickly turned to the woman who had asked about the young man's brother and said, "Do you know this man?"

"Yes, that's Cain," the woman responded, then looked over to the dead body on the ground, then to Cain, who stood there frozen, when a realization hit her, and she vailed out.

"Cain, what have you done to Abel?"

20

ROAD TRIP

In the annals of the insect kingdom, a humble fly found itself unwittingly trapped on the windshield of an ordinary sedan. From its precarious perch, the fly bore witness to the absurd, often exasperating world of human transportation. Little did it know that its journey on this vehicle would be a crash course in the astounding idiocy that prevailed among the people traveling by car, bike, and foot.

The journey began as the engine roared to life and the car pulled out of the driveway. The driver, a bespectacled man with a smartphone screen covering his face, appeared to transform into a recklessly confident multitasker. Oblivious to the fact that their attention should have been on the road, they toggled between emails, text messages, and social media updates, all while navigating through a labyrinth of traffic.

The fly clung to the windshield for dear life as the vehicle weaved in and out of lanes, the horn serving as a continuous symphony of disapproval for fellow motorists. The erratic movements of the car only exacerbated the treacherous position the fly found itself in, much to its dismay.

Observations of pedestrians were equally disheartening. As the car stopped at a crosswalk, a cluster of pedestrians waited for the light to change. However, rather than patiently respecting the signal, one man decided to enact his own daring version of "Frogger," leaping across the road with utter disregard for the concept of traffic lights.

"Green means go, and red means... you know, whatever," he proclaimed to no one in particular as he dodged oncoming cars, forcing the driver of the vehicle to slam on the brakes. The fly watched in disbelief as the man made it safely to the other side, unscathed, while its head throbbed with the abruptness of the stop.

As the journey continued, an alarming trend among cyclists became apparent. Bikers, in their colorful spandex and aerodynamic helmets, appeared to harbor a collective disdain for common sense and safety. They zipped through intersections without regard for traffic signals, blithely swerved around cars, and occasionally treated sidewalks like personal racetracks.

One particularly audacious cyclist decided to use a pedestrian crosswalk to cut in front of the vehicle. The fly clung to the windshield wiper as the car screeched to a halt to avoid catastrophe. The cyclist, displaying no hint of gratitude or remorse, gave the driver a smug look and sped off, leaving a trail of exasperation in his wake.

The streets were not just a playground for audacious drivers and reckless pedestrians but also for a peculiar breed known as "honking enthusiasts." Every slight delay, real or perceived, resulted in a cacophony of angry blares from irate motorists. They honked at each other, at pedestrians, at the weather, and at the very fabric of existence itself. The fly, stuck on the windshield, yearned for a moment of peace amidst the ceaseless symphony of horns.

As the vehicle approached a roundabout, the fly marveled at the baffling choreography of vehicular chaos. Cars entered and exited the circular nightmare with an air of clueless determination, often defying the established rules of right of way, while a lady barely taller than the height of the steering wheel decided to stop while inside to allow vehicles to enter the roundabout. The fly clung to the windshield as the car narrowly avoided collisions with each turn, with the driver muttering incomprehensible curses under their breath.

Pedestrians, too, were not immune to the allure of the round-about. A fearless individual, sporting a sandwich board that read, "Lost Tourist Seeking Adventure," strolled into the midst of the swirling traffic, completely undeterred by the screeching brakes and colorful language.

In the midst of the chaos, the fly often longed for the simplicity of nature. To witness a squirrel dashing across the road or a bird gliding through the air without a care in the world was a dream it held dear. But in this human-made spectacle, chaos reigned supreme.

Suddenly, the fly's plight took a darker turn as rain began to fall. The wipers sprang to life, and the fly braced for the impending deluge. As the driver adjusted the wiper speed, the fly's existence as a fly was wiped away, quite literally, in the blink of an eye. The world became a blur of water and motion, and its brief existence had been an exercise in survival.

As it met its untimely end under the relentless windshield wiper, the fly could not help but wonder if, in the grand scheme of things, it had been the most sensible being on that tumultuous road. But alas, its musings were extinguished, and it found itself relegated to the annals of history as a mere smudge on the glass, a casualty of the ceaseless absurdity of human transportation.

21

EMBERS OF WONDER

Tom sat before the hearth, his gaze fixed on the flickering flames that moved like mystical dancers in a passionate ballet. The five-year-old boy sprawled on the floor, cradling his rosy cheeks in his tiny hands, his elbows propped up like miniature pillars of wonderment. He surrendered himself to the allure of the fire's embrace, feeling its warmth caress his skin like his mother's touch, enveloping him in a cocoon of comfort akin to a downy feather duvet.

Gordon, his father, rose from his chair with deliberate grace, meticulously folding the newspaper before placing it on the nearby table. With a fluid motion, he selected a log from the basket, tossing it into the fire with a flourish that ignited a symphony of sparks. Each spark resembled a miniature firefly, stirring from slumber on a warm summer evening, casting an ethereal glow in the darkness as they searched for their celestial mates.

The wood crackled and popped as the flames hungrily consumed the fresh offering, their voracious appetite demanding more sustenance. The fire roared to life, casting a warm, flickering spotlight upon Gordon's figure as he deftly arranged the logs within the hearth's pit.

"Be mindful of the flames, Tom," Gordon cautioned, his voice a gentle reminder amidst the crackling chorus of the fire. But Tom remained ensnared by the captivating tableau before him, his gaze fixed on the mesmerizing dance of the flames. Within their fiery embrace, he witnessed the ancient dance of life unfolding—the birth of a towering oak from a humble seed, the birds nesting within its protective boughs, and the ever-changing foliage that adorned its branches with each passing season.

In that moment, Tom was not merely a spectator before the hearth; he was a witness to the timeless spectacle of nature's grandeur, captivated by the beauty and mystery that lay within the heart of the flames.

Tom was startled from his reverie when a thought struck him, prompting him to turn to his father with a question.

"May I add paper to the flames?" he inquired.

Gordon, engrossed in reading the Washington Post, responded without raising his gaze. "Yes, but only a small piece," he instructed the boy.

With care, Tom selected a weathered piece of paper from the stack his father had placed beside the logs for nightly kindling. Though he glanced at the paper briefly, its contents remained a mystery to him.

"Dad, what does this say?" he queried, handing the paper to his father.

Gordon's voice resonated as he read aloud, "Gary Powers, the U2 pilot who was shot down by Soviet surface-to-air missiles, has been in prison for over four months."

Tom studied the grainy, black-and-white photograph of the man accused of espionage. With a twist of his hand, he cast the paper into the fire before returning to his place on the floor.

The flames engulfed the paper slowly, consuming the image of the man's face before his very eyes, giving way to a vivid narrative that unfolded like a cinematic reel. He glimpsed Gary Powers as an infant in 1929, born in Kentucky, his family's relocation to Virginia during his childhood, his education at Milligan College, and his subsequent service in the Air Force and CIA. Tom witnessed the moment Powers' U2 plane was downed and his capture by the Soviets, the sequence of events unfolding before him like scenes from a forbidden television series, akin to his father's beloved Twilight Zone. Mesmerized, Tom found himself entranced by this private spectacle hidden in the flickering depths of the flames.

This December night in 1960 was a pivotal moment etched into Tom's childhood memories, as he realized that he possessed a special gift for delving into the lives of others. He pursued tales whispered by others, tales only he could truly witness. Igniting various articles within his father's ashtray, Tom observed with fascination as narratives unfurled amidst the flickering flames. Yet, as the allure of these articles waned, the school library became his next hunting ground, and its books fell victim to his insatiable curiosity.

Unbeknownst to his parents, Tom's voracious appetite for books was not driven by scholarly pursuits but rather by a desire to feed the hungry flames, consuming the pages one by one. Tom's fascination with fire grew as he realized the strong hold it had over his imagination as the fiery inferno devoured each book. In the mesmerizing dance of the flames, Tom found solace—a realm where he wielded control over the stories that unfolded, a sanctuary from the constraints of reality. As the years passed and Tom matured into adulthood, his fascination with fire grew alongside him.

Despite his dreams of becoming a firefighter remaining unfulfilled, Tom pursued a career as a cook, drawn to the proximity of open flames. His penchant for burning pages from recipe books often led to conflicts with his employers, resulting in frequent job changes. Observing a calf maturing on a neighboring farm, only to later become a steak for the local mayor, or witnessing golden wheat swaying in the summer breeze, destined to be transformed into crusty bread, briefly satisfied his hunger. Undeterred, Tom continued to chase his own personal stories within the fiery infernos.

By the turn of the century, Tom's hunger for excitement could no longer be sated by burning mere pages from books and magazines. He began shadowing fire trucks, yet even this pursuit grew stale with time, and Tom sought out new thrills. One night, he sneaked into the neighbor's shed, accidentally igniting a blaze that unleashed a thrill unlike any he had known. The flames danced around him, casting an eerie glow on his face as he watched in awe. The adrenaline rush that followed was intoxicating, leaving him craving more like a junkie looking for his next fix. He unleashed the fierce dragon from within that had been caged for years, and he embarked on a spree of arson across the cityscape, eventually earning the notorious title of the city's most infamous serial arsonist in its history. Tom felt more powerful and alive than ever before. But deep down, a small voice whispered that he was on a path to destruction.

No home was safe in the city as he continued to set fire to building after building, leaving a trail of destruction in his wake. He knew that he could never turn back. The flames were consuming his mind, and there was no way to extinguish them. As the authorities were closing in, he knew that he was running out of time. The fire grew larger as his appetite grew more insatiable and his actions more reckless. He was a slave to the flames, unable to resist their destructive allure. And as he watched the city burn around him, he realized that the stories he chased as a child had become his prison.

But tragedy struck when he was diagnosed with lung cancer. The result of the flames he had spent his life breathing in—the narratives he so desperately clung to—was now suffocating him. Terrified by being bedridden, Tom made one last attempt to see the world that no one else saw. He was standing in the center of an abandoned house, which had only received visits from the neighborhood kids who dared one another to enter. The weed around the home grew tall and wild, entwining around the structure and blocking out the sunlight. There he stood with his eyes closed as he struck a match for the last time. The fire quickly spread around the wooden structure, engulfing everything in its path. As the flames grew higher and hotter, he watched in silence, knowing that this was the end of everything he had ever known. In that moment, the final reel began to play, and Tom's life became the narrative of his own tragic story as he became one with the flames. The crackling of the fire drowned out the sirens surrounding the burning house, leaving only the echoes of what once was in its wake as Tom took his last breath, and became the story itself.

22

FAN MAIL

Esteemed Pontius Pilate,

It is with a mixture of reverence and lamentation that I address you, reflecting upon your tenure as the prefect of Roman-occupied Palestine. Your actions, though undoubtedly impactful, have left a lasting impression upon the tapestry of our shared history, albeit not in the manner one might expect.

Your steadfast dedication to disregarding the religious sensitivities of the Jewish populace is a testament to your unwavering commitment to your own beliefs, albeit at the expense of fostering harmony and understanding among diverse religious communities. Your promotion of Roman religion and emperor worship in a region steeped in centuries-old traditions stands as a stark reminder of the power dynamics at play within the Roman Empire.

Furthermore, your ability to incite unrest and provoke riots among both Jews and Samaritans is a testament to your influence, albeit misguided in its execution. The discord you sowed only served to deepen existing divisions and sow the seeds of future conflict, leaving a legacy of turmoil in your wake.

Lastly, your trial in Rome for cruelty and oppression serves as a sobering reminder of the consequences of unchecked power and the inherent dangers of governance devoid of compassion and empathy. To incur the ire of the very empire you purported to serve is a testament to the gravity of your actions and the ramifications thereof.

In closing, Esteemed Pontius Pilate, though my words may carry an air of sarcasm, they are offered with a measure of admiration for the undeniable impact you have had upon the course of history.

May your legacy serve as a cautionary tale, guiding future leaders towards a governance founded upon principles of compassion and understanding.

With a reflective gaze and a somber tone,
Philo of Alexandria

23

THE BANANA BANDIT

In the vibrant heart of Colombia, amidst the lush tropical jungle and endless rows of towering banana plants, a group of young boys were playing their favorite game. Their laughter echoed through the plantation, a symphony of joy and innocence. The sun shone brightly overhead, casting playful shadows on the rich, dark soil. The boys, all around the age of six, had divided into two groups, each led by a charismatic leader. This wasn't just any game; it was a fierce battle for the most coveted prize: the golden bananas.

"Viva los plátanos!" shouted the leader of the first group, his eyes gleaming with excitement. His name was Pablo, though the name held little significance to anyone yet. Pablo had a quick wit and an even quicker smile, traits that made him both a beloved friend and a formidable opponent. From a young age, he had a knack for strategy and an innate understanding of human nature, skills that would serve him in ways the world could not yet imagine.

On the other side, the leader of the rival group, Anton, raised his stick high. "We'll never let you take our bananas, Pablo!" he declared with a defiant grin. Anton was Pablo's best friend, but in this game, they were sworn enemies.

The boys had crafted makeshift weapons from branches and leaves, their imaginations transforming them into swords and shields. They hid behind the banana plants, their eyes peering through the green foliage, planning their next move.

Pablo turned to his loyal comrades, whispering, "We need a new strategy. If we keep attacking head-on, they'll see us coming every time."

One of his friends, a boy named Mateo, nodded eagerly. "What if we go around the back? There's a path through the tall grass that leads right to their stash."

Pablo considered this, then shook his head. "No, they'll expect that. But I have another idea." He leaned in closer, lowering his voice. "I'll go and talk to Anton. I'll pretend we want to make an alliance and share the bananas. While we're talking, you sneak in and take as many as you can carry."

Mateo's eyes widened. "But what if they catch us?"

Pablo's grin turned mischievous. "They won't. Trust me."

With the plan set, Pablo stepped out into the open, hands raised in a gesture of peace. "Anton! Let's talk."

Anton appeared from behind a thick cluster of banana plants, his eyes narrowing in suspicion. "What do you want, Pablo?"

Pablo approached slowly, his smile disarming. "We've been fighting all morning. Maybe it's time we worked together instead. Think about it: if we join forces, we can gather more bananas than we could ever imagine."

Anton's frown softened. "You really mean that?"

Pablo nodded earnestly. "Of course. We're best friends, right? We should be on the same side."

Anton glanced back at his group, who were watching the exchange with bated breath. After a moment, he extended his hand. "Okay, deal."

As they shook hands, Pablo could see Mateo and the others creeping towards Anton's stash. He kept Anton distracted, talking about all the adventures they could have together with their combined haul of bananas.

"Just think," Pablo said, his voice low and persuasive, "we could be the kings of the plantation. No one would dare challenge us."

Anton's eyes sparkled with excitement at the thought. "You're right, Pablo. Together, we'd be unstoppable."

But as soon as Mateo and the others had their arms full of bananas, Pablo's smile faded. He pulled his hand away from Anton's grip. "Sorry, Anton," he said, a hint of regret in his voice. "But all's fair in war."

Before Anton could react, Pablo turned and ran, shouting to his friends, "Now! Go, go, go!"

Chaos erupted as Anton's group realized they had been deceived. They chased after Pablo and his friends, but it was too late. Pablo's group had already disappeared into the dense banana plants, their laughter echoing through the plantation.

Breathless and triumphant, Pablo looked back at his friends, their arms laden with bananas. "We did it," he panted. "We won."

Mateo grinned. "You're a genius, Pablo."

As they sat in the shade of the banana plants, feasting on their hard-won prize, Pablo couldn't help but feel a pang of guilt. He looked at Anton, who was watching them from a distance, his expression a mix of betrayal and admiration.

Pablo waved him over. "Come on, Anton. There's enough for everyone."

Anton hesitated, then slowly made his way over, a reluctant smile spreading across his face. "You're a real bandit, you know that?"

Pablo laughed, offering him a banana. "Maybe. But I'm still your best friend, right?"

Anton took the banana and nodded. "Always."

As the sun began to set over the plantation, casting long shadows across the rows of banana plants, the boys sat together, their rivalry forgotten, their friendship stronger than ever. Little did they know that one of them would one day become known far and wide.

Years passed, and the game of the banana plantation became a distant memory. But the traits that Pablo exhibited as a child only grew sharper with age. His quick wit turned into cunning, his strategic mind into a powerful tool of manipulation, and his charisma into a means of control. He learned to exploit the trust of others, just as he had done with Anton, to achieve his goals.

Even in his teenage years, Pablo's ambition was clear. He started small, selling contraband cigarettes and fake lottery tickets. But he dreamed bigger. The banana plantation where he once played now served as a backdrop to his burgeoning empire. He began to involve himself in more lucrative ventures, always staying one step ahead of the law, just as he had stayed one step ahead of Anton and his friends.

One day, as they sat under the shade of the banana plants, Anton voiced his concerns. "Pablo, don't you think we're getting in too deep? This isn't just child's play anymore."

Pablo shrugged, a sly smile playing on his lips. "Relax, Anton. We've got it all under control. Besides, the money is good. Don't you like living comfortably?"

Anton sighed. "It's not about the money, Pablo. It's about what we're doing. We're hurting people."

Pablo's eyes darkened. "Sometimes you have to do bad things to get ahead, Anton. It's just the way the world works."

Anton looked at him, a mixture of sadness and fear in his eyes. "I don't know if I can keep doing this, Pablo."

Pablo's smile faded. "You're either with me or against me, Anton. Make your choice."

Pablo's childhood friends, including Anton, were never far from his thoughts. He often enlisted them in his schemes, knowing they trusted him implicitly. Anton, loyal to a fault, followed Pablo into the darker realms of their small-time criminal activities, never fully realizing the extent of Pablo's ambitions.

One evening, as the sun dipped below the horizon, casting an orange glow over the plantation, Pablo and Anton sat on a fallen log, reminiscing about their childhood games.

"Remember the time we played war over the bananas?" Anton asked, chuckling. "You tricked me good that day."

Pablo smirked, a hint of something darker in his eyes. "I was always thinking ahead. Even then, I knew how to get what I wanted."

Anton shook his head, still smiling. "You were always the smart one, Pablo."

Pablo's expression softened for a moment. "And you were always the loyal one, Anton. I couldn't have done half of what I've accomplished without you."

Anton's smile faltered slightly, sensing an underlying tension in Pablo's words. "We're a team, right? Like always."

"Of course," Pablo said, clapping a hand on Anton's shoulder. "Like always."

Pablo's rise to power was swift and ruthless. He moved from petty crimes to smuggling operations and, eventually, to the drug trade. His charm and strategic mind made him a natural leader, but it was his willingness to deceive and betray that set him apart. He built an empire on the backs of those who trusted him, manipulating alliances and eliminating rivals with the same ease with which he had once tricked Anton.

The once idyllic banana plantation, where boys played and laughed, now bore silent witness to Pablo's transformation. The lush greenery, the same plants that had hidden Pablo's friends during their childhood games, now concealed more sinister activities. Trucks laden with illicit goods rumbled through the narrow paths, and armed men patrolled the area, ensuring the smooth operation of Pablo's burgeoning empire.

One day, as Pablo sat in silence on the porch, overlooking the land that had shaped his childhood and his future, Anton approached him, a troubled look on his face.

"Pablo, things are getting out of hand," Anton said quietly. "People are getting hurt. This isn't what we dreamed of as kids."

Pablo turned to him, his expression hardening. "Dreams change, Anton. We're not kids anymore. This is our reality now."

"But at what cost?" Anton persisted. "We've lost friends. People are scared of you."

Pablo's eyes flashed with a mixture of anger and disappointment. "Fear is a tool, Anton. It keeps people in line. It keeps us in power."

Anton looked at him, a sadness in his eyes that Pablo hadn't seen before. "I don't recognize you anymore, Pablo. The boy I knew wouldn't have done this."

Pablo's expression softened for a brief moment. "Maybe that boy never existed, Anton. Maybe this was who I was meant to be all along."

Anton shook his head, stepping back. "I can't be part of this anymore, Pablo. I can't keep betraying who I am."

Pablo watched as Anton walked away, but he felt nothing. The Banana Bandit he once was had long vanished, replaced by the King of Cocaine, a man driven by ambition and a thirst for power. As Anton's figure grew smaller in the distance, Pablo's hand tightened around the cold steel of his gun.

With a resolve hardened by years of ruthless decisions, he raised the weapon, aiming at the back of his once best friend. The shot rang out, echoing through the forest. Birds scattered from the canopy as Anton crumpled to the ground, a silent testament to the end of their friendship and the boyhood dreams that had long since faded.

Pablo approached the fallen figure and stood over Anton, watching the life drain from his best friend's eyes. "I win, Anton. I always win."

The plantation, with its lush banana plants and sun-dappled paths, remained a silent witness to the transformation of a boy into a man, of innocence into infamy. As the shadows grew longer each day, the echoes of laughter and the memories of childhood games lingered, a poignant reminder of what was lost in the relentless pursuit of power.

24

MIDNIGHT REVERIE

Nathan tossed and turned in bed, his movements careful and slow as he reached for his phone from the nightstand. The digital screen lit up the dark room, cruelly revealing the time: 3:22 a.m. With a heavy sigh, he put the device back down, its light casting faint, ghostly shapes on the walls.

Sleep had become an elusive friend for Nathan over the years, slipping through his grasp like water through his fingers. Each night melded into the next, an unyielding cycle of insomnia that tormented his restless mind. Like a relentless worm gnawing at the core of an apple, his thoughts consumed him from within, eroding any chance of finding solace in the comfort of dreams.

Nathan, a single, middle-aged man, found himself residing in the basement of his parents' house—a stark contrast to the bustling life he led on Wall Street. Here, surrounded by relics of his teenage years, the poorly lit room served as both sanctuary and reminder of the harsh realities he faced. Despite his success in the financial world, Nathan's personal life had borne the brunt of broken relationships and the unrelenting demands of a high-pressure job. The weight of loneliness bore down on him daily, a burden he carried in stoic silence. His parents, unaware of the depth of his emotional turmoil, offered well-intentioned but ultimately hollow attempts at comfort.

In the solitude of his basement sanctuary, Nathan grappled with memories on yet another sleepless night. Echoes of lost love and missed opportunities haunted him, their whispers mingling with the relentless pressures of his career. The frenetic pace of Wall Street allowed no respite, leaving him physically and emotionally drained. As the night dragged on, Nathan lay in bed, the weight of past and present bearing down on him like an anchor. With each passing moment, he yearned for a glimmer of hope to pierce the darkness enveloping his life. Yet, amidst the silence, the solution remained elusive, lost in the tempestuous sea of his thoughts.

Nathan's daily ritual of consuming countless energy drinks aimed to keep him alert and focused, but it only served to exacerbate his insomnia. Each day blurred into the next, and each night blurred into day, leaving him fixated on thoughts of sleep rather than the fluctuating stock prices on his screen. His boss offered no respite, only relentless demands. Nathan found himself scrutinized for productivity and often chastised for falling short of his peers, trapped in a cycle of exhaustion and anxiety. The relentless pressure to excel at work compounded his sleeplessness, plunging him deeper into mental and physical fatigue.

As night descended, Nathan's body pleaded for rest, yet his mind persisted in its ceaseless examination of his life's trajectory. The nocturnal hours became a stage for introspection as Nathan grappled with his innermost thoughts, his body gently urging him to heed the call of his natural rhythms. In the midst of another sleepless night, Nathan found himself contemplating a colleague's suggestion to try meditation as a pre-sleep ritual. Grounded in pragmatism and skepticism of mystical methods, he reluctantly turned to his phone, embarking on a late-night internet search. It was then he stumbled upon the website of Dr. Erik Johansson, a renowned Swedish psychologist celebrated for his mastery in hypnosis. Promising the improbable prospect of achieving a truly restful night's sleep, Dr. Johansson's online platform offered a glimmer of hope in Nathan's quest for peace. Without hesitation, he purchased the audio package, his excitement mounting as it painstakingly downloaded onto his phone. With earphones in place, he clicked play, eagerly immersing himself in the narrator's soothing voice.

"Slowly inhale," the voice intoned, "feel the air fill your lungs. Exhale through your nose, pausing briefly in the moment when breath escapes you. You are calm. Your body grows heavy, sinking into the bed with each exhalation."

As Nathan's alarm blared at 7 a.m., he could not shake the surreal feeling that enveloped him. Was he still in the realm of the living, or had he slipped into an otherworldly dimension? With newfound optimism and the blessing of a restful night's sleep, Nathan was certain he had found the solution to his problem and embraced his newfound belief. Night after night, Nathan found solace in Dr. Johansson's soothing voice, feeling increasingly rejuvenated. He yearned for it throughout the day, eagerly anticipating the arrival of nightfall. He found comfort in the quiet moments of the night, embracing the stillness and tranquility that surrounded him. The nights promised him the escape he so desperately sought—away from the chaos and noise of the world—but above all, the deep sleep that seemed out of reach for years.

As the days passed, Nathan's confidence grew as he felt more energized and focused. With Dr. Johansson's guidance, he was able to conquer his fears and face each day with a newfound sense of purpose and determination. Nathan never felt better, and he was more at peace with himself than ever before. The past no longer troubled him, and he finally understood his purpose.

One warm summer morning, Nathan followed his usual routine of going to work. However, instead of heading to his desk, he walked directly into his boss's office. There, he paused briefly, meeting the man's gaze in silence, then, with a sense of determination, he reached into his pocket and pulled out his resignation letter.

"I'm in control of my own destiny," Nathan said as he handed over the folded paper.

Moments later, in a tragic turn of events, Nathan took his own life with a knife retrieved from his backpack, in front of everyone present. The immediate severance of his artery resulted in blood spraying across the office glass, eliciting screams of disbelief from the women and leaving the men frozen in shock as Nathan's final moments played out in agonizing slow motion before their eyes.

No one understood. No one believed. Everyone knew that Nathan was a changed man, but for the better. His suicide was an unpredicted tragedy. When the police retrieved his phone, the audio was still playing through his headphones as his last words echoed in the empty room.

"Slowly inhale and feel the air expanding your lungs. Breathe out through your nose and pause for a short while, concentrating on the single moment when you're not breathing. You're calm. Your body feels heavy, sinking into the bed with each breath. Imagine that you're walking on the beach, with gentle waves caressing the shores.

The sun is setting on the horizon, painting the sky and the water beneath it red.

The sound of the waves crashing against the sand fills your ears, bringing a sense of peace and tranquility. You take a deep breath and let all your worries drift away with the tide. You find a boat tethered to a nearby dock and decide to take it out onto the open water. As you row further away from the shore, the only sound you hear is the gentle lapping of the water against the boat. The warm breeze brushes against your skin, carrying with it a sense of freedom and

serenity. Imagine that you're the solution to your problems. You're in control of your own destiny."

185

25

THE CASSEROLE QUEEN

In the heart of 1953 Savannah, Georgia, lived Mrs. Terry Tibbits, a plump and vivacious 50-something housewife with a knack for whipping up tantalizing casseroles. With her fiery red hair and charming southern drawl, she commanded attention in the kitchen. Her dream? To clinch the title of Casserole Queen at the upcoming state fair. But fate had a different dish in mind.

As Terry delved into uncharted culinary territory, a deadly mistake brewed beneath her apron. What she thought was a harmless parsnip turned out to be hemlock, a poisonous plant that would bring about a tragedy she never saw coming.

Terry's excitement turned to horror when her beloved husband, Toby Tibbits, fell gravely ill after tasting her latest creation. As he succumbed to the effects of the hemlock, Terry's world unraveled. Panic set in as she realized her inadvertent role in his demise. Frantically, she covered her tracks, desperate to hide the truth.

Terry's culinary world had always been her solace, a place where she could lose herself in the rich aromas and comforting routines. Her casseroles were legendary at every potluck in the city. Her kitchen was her sanctuary, adorned with family heirlooms and the latest gadgets that Toby had lovingly bought for her. But as Toby lay dying, the walls of her sanctuary seemed to close in, the comforting smells now mingling with the acrid stench of fear.

Toby Tibbits, a kind-hearted man with a penchant for fishing, had been Terry's steadfast companion for over thirty years. His gentle nature and unwavering support had been the cornerstones of her life. As he gasped for breath, Terry's mind raced back to the simple joys they shared—picnics by the river, evenings on the porch, and the way he always said her casseroles were the best he'd ever tasted. The realization that she was losing him and that she was responsible shattered her.

But fate, it seems, had other plans. Enter Elizabeth Whitaker, a wealthy socialite with secrets of her own. Elizabeth, with her elegant dresses and a sharp wit hidden behind a polished smile, had long suspected her husband of infidelity. When she confided in Terry about her suspicions, a deadly alliance was born. Terry's culinary skills became her weapon, and the wives of the wealthy elite became her clientele. Casseroles were baked, and money kept coming in from the grieving widows of Savannah.

Elizabeth's background was as colorful as her social gatherings. Born into old money, she was known for her extravagant parties and sharp tongue. Her marriage to Robert Whitaker, a prominent businessman, was the talk of the town—not for its romance, but for its convenience. Robert's wandering eye had been a well-kept secret until Elizabeth decided it was time to take control. Her alliance with Terry was not born out of desperation but out of a calculated move to protect her status and wealth.

Terry's enterprise flourished, and so did the whispers of suspicion. The local police chief, her late husband's boss, began to take a keen interest in her activities, sensing that something sinister lurked beneath the surface of her seemingly innocent casseroles.

Chief William Patterson had seen it all in his thirty years on the force. A decorated war veteran with a keen sense of justice, he was a man of few words but deep convictions. Toby's death had struck a chord with him, not just because Toby had been a good officer, but because Patterson had promised to look after Terry. His suspicions grew as he noticed the increasing number of sudden deaths among Savannah's elite. But who could be behind it all? Chief Patterson confided his concerns to Terry over a refreshing glass of iced tea on the porch one hot summer afternoon. Little did he know—it was a deadly mistake.

Faced with the threat of exposure, Terry knew she had to act fast. With a heavy heart and a steady hand, she concocted her most daring scheme yet. The Savannah Chief of Police, a man who had once been her husband's mentor, would now become her next target.

Under the guise of grief and gratitude, Terry approached the chief with a casserole laced with a lethal dose of hemlock. As he savored each mouthful, unaware of the danger lurking within, Terry watched with bated breath.

Days passed, and Terry's anxiety mounted as she waited for news of her latest victim. Finally, word came—Patterson had been found dead in his home, the victim of what appeared to be a sudden heart attack.

With the chief now out of the picture, Terry breathed a sigh of relief. But her victory was short-lived. As whispers of foul play grew louder, the eyes of suspicion turned squarely in her direction. The local rookie detective, fueled by a gut feeling and a determination to uncover the truth, began to dig deeper into Mrs. Tibbits' past.

Detective James Edwards was fresh out of the academy, eager to prove himself. His sharp mind and relentless curiosity had made him top of his class. Assigned to the unsolved cases, Edwards could not shake the feeling that Chief Patterson's death was not of natural causes. Edwards meticulously pieced together the clues, from the unusual increase in wealthy widows to the common thread of Terry's casseroles.

Caught between a desire for freedom and the fear of being caught, Terry Tibbits found herself at a crossroads. Would she continue down the path of deception, risking everything for the sake of her deadly enterprise? Or would she finally face the consequences of her actions and seek redemption for the lives she had taken?

As the net of justice closed in around Terry Tibbits, she found herself in a precarious position. The young detective's suspicions grew stronger with each passing day, and Terry knew that her days as the Casserole Queen were numbered. But just when it seemed that all hope was lost, an unexpected lifeline emerged from the shadows.

Her clientele of wealthy wives, whose husbands had met untimely ends at Terry's hand, rallied to her side. Recognizing the imminent threat to their own reputations and freedom, they devised a daring plan to shift the blame onto another unsuspecting wife—one who had long been the target of their disdain.

Under the cover of darkness, the group of conspirators set their plan into motion. They planted false evidence linking the murders to their unwitting scapegoat, manipulating the scene to incriminate her beyond a shadow of a doubt.

As the investigation unfolded, suspicion fell squarely on the unsuspecting wife, her life torn apart by accusations of crimes she had never committed. And as the evidence mounted against her, Terry Tibbits watched from the sidelines, hoping for a conviction. Edwards, however was not easily convinced.

But even as the plan unfolded, cracks began to form in the facade of unity among the wealthy wives. Tensions simmered beneath the surface, threatening to unravel their carefully constructed web of deception. And as the truth threatened to emerge, Terry Tibbits realized that the consequences of her actions would not be so easily erased.

In the end, justice would prevail—but at what cost? For Terry Tibbits and the wealthy wives of Savannah, the road to redemption would be paved with lies, deceit, and the bitter taste of betrayal. And as the dust settled on their tangled web of secrets, they would be forced to confront the true price of their ambition.

But Terry had other plans than getting caught. Under the guise of reconciliation and an attempt at covert operations, Terry extended an invitation to Edwards for a private dinner at her home. Unbeknownst to him, the table was set with the very casserole that had been her weapon of choice—a delectable fish casserole laced with the deadly ingredient that had claimed so many lives.

As the detective prepared to savor the meal, Terry observed from a distance, her anticipation palpable. Yet, fate intervened—or was it the detective's calculated strategy? As he served himself a portion of the casserole, a piece slipped from his grasp, landing on the floor with a fateful clatter.

In an unforeseen turn of events, Terry's beloved cat, Toby, a faithful tabby companion matching her fiery hair, seized the fallen morsel and devoured it with unsuspecting gusto. Within moments, the lethal effects of the poisoned dish took hold, leaving both Terry and the detective transfixed in a mixture of shock and horror.

With the evidence now irrefutable, the detective moved swiftly to apprehend Terry Tibbits, the once-revered Casserole Queen of Savannah. As the truth of her crimes came to light, the city was rocked by the revelation of the century—a tale of deceit, betrayal, and culinary cunning that had ensnared them all.

Upon her arrest, the grieving widows swiftly distanced themselves from Terry, condemning her for the heinous act of murdering their beloved husbands and returning to enjoying their afternoons at the Country Club.

As for the detective, he emerged as the unsung hero of the saga—a beacon of truth in a world shrouded in darkness. And as the sun set on the streets of Savannah, the memory of the Casserole

Queen faded into legend, a cautionary tale of the dangers that lurk beneath the surface of even the most delectable dishes.

26

RESORT DIARIES

Day 1

Well, this is quite an unexpected turn of events. I was just minding my own business and going about my day when I suddenly found myself at this new resort. It's certainly a far cry from the vacation I'd planned in Hawaii, but who am I to complain? My father must have planned this surprise vacation, for sure! He's well known to play jokes on everyone. The transportation wasn't very upscale, but they gave me a nice uniform to wear! Stripes are so in this season. The staff here seems a bit stern, but I suppose they're just very dedicated to their jobs. And the other guests—well, let's just say they're a bit rough around the edges.

Day 2

Today was quite eventful! They have some interesting activities here. I participated in a "mandatory exercise" session this morning.

It was essentially a brisk jog around a large courtyard, but with lots of enthusiastic shouting from the staff. They even provide personal trainers who make sure you don't slack off! It's like a fitness boot camp. Tall, imposing fences with barbed wire surround the courtyard itself—quite a unique architectural choice for a resort.

I tried to make friends with a few of the other guests, but they seemed rather reserved. There was one particularly burly guy with tattoos all over his arms who gave me a long, hard stare when I asked him how long he'd been here. Maybe they just need some time to warm up to me.

Day 3

I must admit, the food here leaves much to be desired. It's a bit bland, and the portions are small. I'm starting to think this place is more of a health spa, considering the low-calorie meals. I miss my daily cappuccino and bagel. Instead, I had some kind of mystery meat for lunch. The culinary adventure continues! The dining hall is a large, echoey space with long tables and benches, reminiscent of a school cafeteria.

The staff also insisted on showing us our "accommodations" in more detail today. My room has minimalistic decor. The designer was either Japanese or Swedish. I saw magazines like that, although those rooms looked nicer in the pictures. The bed's hard, the pillow's thin, and the walls are cold concrete. My roommate, Big Mike, is a bit of a grump. He doesn't talk much; he just grunts and occasionally gives me a rather intense look. I'm sure we'll become best friends in no time!

Day 4

Today I discovered the most interesting thing: they have a communal shower here. It's like a throwback to my high school gym days! It's a bit awkward, but I suppose it's all part of the experience. The showers are lined up against the wall with no dividers, and there's staff standing at the entrance, watching us.

The other guests don't seem to appreciate my attempts at conversation, though. One even told me to "shut up" in a rather rude manner. His name is Gonzo, and he has a distinctive tattoo of a snake wrapped around a dagger on his arm. Big Mike later told me that Gonzo is part of some South American group. It's just another hurdle to making friends, I guess.

I also noticed they keep quite a strict schedule here—lights out at 10 PM sharp. It's refreshing to have such a structured routine. I haven't had this kind of discipline since… well, ever. It must be a boot camp, but to be fair, they ought to feed us better.

Day 5

I'm starting to think this place is less of a resort and more of a… what's the word? Institution? I overheard some of the guests talking about their "sentences" and "parole hearings." Maybe it's a legal retreat? That would explain the uniforms and the stern staff. I should've paid more attention to the fine print when I signed the paperwork.

Today, I attended a group meeting where everyone shared their stories. It was very touching, although most of them seemed to have a criminal twist. I shared my own story about getting lost on my way to Hawaii and ending up here. They seemed to find it quite amusing, though I'm not entirely sure why. One of the men, Dolfie, who is apparently part of an Aryan team, gave me a knowing look. Big Mike told me later that Dolfie is someone you definitely want to stay on the good side of.

Day 6

Today I finally had a proper conversation with my roommate. His name is Big Mike, and he's actually quite friendly once you get past the gruff exterior. He told me more about some of the other guests here and the group programs they run for the residents. Other than the South American group Gonzo is part of and the strange group called "Aryan," Dolfie seems to lead; Big Mike said there's another called Crips. It's fantastic that we have these programs here. I'm sure I can find a prospectus on it somewhere.

Big Mike did warn me to stay on Dolfie's good side. Apparently, he's the guy to go to if you need anything from "outside." I don't know what he meant by that, but I'm intrigued. I need to ask him about his odd tattoos next time I see him. What possessed him to ink his neck with what looks like broken twigs arranged in a strange shape—only he knows. Speaking of which, Gonzo's tattoos, on the other hand, are filled with numbers. I wonder if those were his winning lottery numbers.

I also attended another mandatory exercise session today. I'm starting to appreciate these workouts; they really help pass the time and keep me in shape. The personal trainers are very motivational. The gym is a stark, gray room with weights and old, squeaky machines. It's not exactly Gold's Gym, but it does the job. I'm starting to like this boot camp.

Day 7

This place is definitely not a resort. Today, during another group meeting, one of the guests referred to our stay here as "doing time." I had a sudden epiphany—I'm in prison! That explains everything: the uniforms, the stern staff, the strict schedule, the communal showers. What the hell?

I shared my revelation with Big Mike, Gonzo, and Dolfie. They had a good laugh at my expense but were surprisingly supportive. Big Mike even said, "Welcome to reality, kid." Gonzo offered to show me around properly, and Dolfie said he could get me any-thing I needed—for a price, of course.

It's starting to sink in now. This isn't the vacation I planned, but it's the one I've got. And if I'm going to be here for a while, I might as well make the best of it. Evidently, I have 11,248 more days to go.

27

ART FOOLERY

Welcome to a satirical journey through the epochs of art, where each era unfolds with its own brand of eccentricity and flair. From the primal canvases of prehistoric caves to the exaggerated opulence of Baroque extravagance, and from the geometric austerity of Bauhaus to the perplexing depths of contemporary art, prepare to witness art history through a lens of playful irreverence. Join me as we traverse through time, where art isn't just a reflection of human creativity but a humorous exploration of our ever-changing perceptions and pretensions.

Prehistoric art:

The original masterpiece collection! Imagine a world where cavemen and women, armed with nothing but crude tools and boundless creativity, turned rugged cave walls into their personal canvases. From the iconic cave paintings of Lascaux to the enigmatic petroglyphs etched into stone, these early artists were the OG trendsetters, setting the stage for millennia of artistic expression to come.

Forget about high-definition screens and fancy brushes—prehistoric artists had a refreshingly raw approach to their craft. Using pigments derived from crushed minerals, charcoal, and yes, even spit (because why not?), they brought their visions to life in vibrant hues on the most unlikely of surfaces.

And let's not overlook their subject matter: majestic beasts like woolly mammoths and saber-toothed tigers, immortalized in stunning detail (given the challenge of painting by firelight). So, the next time you find yourself admiring a modern masterpiece in a climate-controlled gallery, take a moment to tip your imaginary hat to these OG artists. Prehistoric art is where caveman chic meets timeless elegance, proving that sometimes simplicity truly is timeless.

Ancient Rome

Ancient Rome: where togas met talent and marble met mischief! Picture a bustling cityscape adorned with larger-than-life statues of emperors in striking poses that would make even the most seasoned Instagram influencer green with envy.

From grandiose monuments to intricate mosaics adorning opulent villas, the Romans knew how to make a statement—and boy, did they do it with flair.

But let's not overlook the cheeky side of Roman art. Imagine stumbling upon a mosaic where a mischievous god pulls pranks on unsuspecting mortals, or a fresco depicting a banquet so raucous that even the wine seems to have a personality of its own.

And those Roman sculptures—oh, the drama! With their theatrical facial expressions and exaggerated gestures, these statues were the ancient equivalent of a melodramatic soap opera, capturing every juicy moment for posterity.

Yet perhaps the most delightful aspect of Roman art was its knack for poking fun at authority. Satirical graffiti mocking pompous politicians, comical caricatures of haughty aristocrats—the Romans knew how to use art to lampoon the powers that be.

So, the next time you wander through the ruins of ancient Rome, take a moment to appreciate the wit and whimsy woven into its art. Because when it comes to humor, the Romans were truly masters of the craft, proving that even empires can have a sense of humor.

Italian Renaissance

The Italian Renaissance, where art, culture, and a healthy dose of drama collided like a Renaissance painting come to life! Picture this: a bustling marketplace filled with merchants haggling over the price of silk, while nearby, a group of intellectuals engage in a heated debate about the merits of Plato versus Aristotle.

But let's not forget the artists—the true rockstars of the Renaissance! From Michelangelo's epic battles with scaffolding to Leonardo da Vinci's never-ending quest to paint the perfect smile, these creative geniuses were like the original influencers, setting trends and turning heads wherever they went.

And then there were the patrons—those wealthy nobles and power-hungry popes who commissioned art like it was going out of style (spoiler alert: it wasn't). With pockets deeper than the Grand Canal, they spared no expense in their quest to outdo one another with ever more lavish displays of wealth and opulence.

But amidst all the grandeur and extravagance, there was a playful side to the Renaissance as well. From bawdy jokes hidden in frescoes to risqué sonnets penned by lovestruck poets, the era was filled with moments of humor and irreverence that added a touch of levity to an otherwise serious affair.

So next time you find yourself wandering the streets of Florence or gazing upon the Sistine Chapel, take a moment to appreciate the laughter woven into the fabric of the Italian Renaissance. Because when it comes to art and entertainment, those Renaissance Italians knew how to put on a show!

Baroque

Baroque art, where drama was as extra as the frills on a powdered wig! Picture this: a grandiose palace dripping with gold leaf and adorned with enough cherubs to give Cupid a run for his money. From extravagant cathedrals to opulent paintings bursting with emotion, the Baroque era was like a theatrical production on canvas.

But let's talk about those paintings—oh, the melodrama! From brooding saints with pensive stares to over-the-top battle scenes straight out of a Hollywood blockbuster, Baroque artists had a flair for the dramatic that would make even Shakespeare blush.

And then there were the sculptures—marble masterpieces that seemed to levitate with their intricate details and gravity-defying poses. It was as if every statue was engaged in a high-stakes game of "how many angels can dance on the head of a pin" (spoiler alert: the answer is always more than you would expect).

But amidst all the pomp and circumstance, there was a playful side to Baroque art as well. Hidden symbols and secret messages are tucked away in paintings, like Easter eggs waiting to be discovered by eagle-eyed art historians.

So next time you find yourself admiring a Baroque masterpiece, take a moment to appreciate the sheer theatricality of it all. Because when it comes to art that packs a punch, Baroque is the undisputed heavyweight champion of the world.

Realism

The Realism movement, where artists traded their rose-tinted glasses for magnifying glasses, and said, "Let's get real!" Imagine a gallery full of meticulously rendered paintings so lifelike that you could almost reach out and take a bite of the fruit in the still life or feel the weight of the oppressed peasants' heavy loads.

And don't forget about capturing hard labor. Ilya Repin's Barge Haulers on the Volga (1873) just makes me want to crawl back to bed and feel grateful for my office job.

But let's talk about those portraits—oh, the realism!

From every wrinkle and crease to each stray hair perfectly rendered, Realist artists were like the OG Instagram hashtag #nofilter, capturing every imperfection and flaw with unflinching honesty.

And then there were the landscapes—scenes so lifelike, you could practically smell the freshly mown grass or feel the cool breeze rustling through the trees. It was like stepping into a Bob Ross painting, minus the happy little trees and with a healthy dose of gritty reality instead.

But amidst all the meticulous attention to detail, there was a playful side to Realism as well. Hidden jokes and subtle nods to the absurdities of everyday life are tucked away in the corners of otherwise straightforward compositions.

So next time you find yourself face-to-face with a Realist masterpiece, take a moment to appreciate the humor and humanity woven into every brushstroke. Because when it comes to keeping it real, Realism takes the cake—and paints it with exquisite precision.

Bauhaus

Bauhaus—the art movement that made geometry cool before it was cool! Picture this: a classroom filled with students meticulously measuring angles and debating the merits of form versus function, all while wearing avant-garde outfits that would make Lady Gaga blush. From stark white walls to minimalist furniture that looked like it was straight out of an IKEA catalog, Bauhaus was like the original hipster haven.

The paintings had nothing short of angles and clean design either. All the drama of the Renaissance disappeared into a 90-degree angle. We cannot help but appreciate Mona Lisa's secret smile, but we also cannot stop and wonder what this masterpiece would look like if created during the Bauhaus era.

But let's talk about those buildings—marvel at the Bauhaus architecture! From sleek skyscrapers to avant-garde homes that looked more like geometric sculptures than places to live, Bauhaus architects were like the Frank Lloyd Wrights of their time, pushing the boundaries of design and daring us to think outside the box. And then there were the art installations—abstract sculptures that seemed to defy gravity and challenge our preconceived notions of what art could be. It was as if the artists were saying, "Forget about traditional painting and sculpture—let us make something that's equal parts mind-bending and thought-provoking!"

But amidst all the avant-garde experimentation, there was a playful side to Bauhaus as well. Hidden jokes and tongue-in-cheek references are tucked away in otherwise serious compositions, like a secret handshake for those in the know. So next time you find yourself admiring a Bauhaus masterpiece, take a moment to appreciate the humor and ingenuity woven into every line and curve. Because when it comes to pushing the boundaries of art and design, Bauhaus was the ultimate trendsetter—and it did it all with style!

Contemporary

Ah, contemporary art, where anything goes and everything is up for interpretation! Picture this: a gallery filled with installations that make you scratch your head in confusion and wonder if you accidentally stumbled into a storage room instead.

From avant-garde sculptures made of everyday objects to paintings that look like someone spilled a can of paint and called it a masterpiece, contemporary art is like a never-ending game of "guess what the artist was thinking."

But let's talk about those performances—oh, the contemporary art performances! From artists pretending to be living statues to interactive exhibits that leave you questioning the meaning of life, contemporary art events are like the weirdest carnival you've ever been to, complete with popcorn and a side of existential crisis.

And then there's the art itself—abstract, absurd, and often absurdly expensive. It's as if the artists are saying, "Who needs skill and technique when you have a concept?" It's like the Emperor's New Clothes of the art world—everyone pretends to understand it but secretly wonders if they are missing something.

But amidst all the confusion and head-scratching, there's a certain charm to contemporary art—a rebellious spirit that says, "Forget the rules, let's make something weird and wonderful." So next time you find yourself face-to-face with a contemporary masterpiece, embrace the absurdity and let yourself be swept away on a journey of artistic exploration. After all, in the world of contemporary art, anything is possible, and that is what makes it so delightfully bizarre.

28

SOLSTICE

In the dimly lit corridors of the Saint-Paul Asylum in Saint-Rémy, two men found solace in each other's company amidst the solitude of their confinement. Here, thick with the scent of oil paint and turpentine, the walls whispered tales of despair and longing. In the summer of 1889, while much of Paris was drunk on absinthe, chasing the green fairy through Montmartre, the French countryside provided a welcome refuge for tormented souls in need of escape. In Saint-Rémy, time seemed to dance to the rhythm of the sun, orchestrating a symphony of golden hues that painted the countryside in hues of amber and honey.

A ginger-haired man with a gaunt face and eyes that held a storm spent his days by the window, his fingers dancing over canvases that only he could understand. His companion, a former professor with a sharp mind dulled by the fog of melancholy, watched in silent fascination. As the days turned into weeks, their bond grew stronger, forged by a shared passion for art and a mutual understanding of the demons that haunted their souls. Together, they found solace in the beauty of the countryside and in the silent companionship they offered each other.

They spoke little, but those conversations were deep, often meandering through the philosophies of life, art, and the nature of madness. The painter, as the professor came to call him, had a peculiar intensity about him, a passion that flared with each stroke of a brush. He often spoke of capturing the essence of the world around him, of distilling its beauty and pain onto canvas.

Over the months as they basked in each other's silence, the professor grew accustomed to the painter's presence and sudden bursts of fervent discourse. They never knew each other's names, for names held little significance in a place where identity was often lost and forgotten.

One evening, as the painter gazed out of the asylum window, his eyes caught sight of the gathering storm on the horizon. The summer night sky darkened, clouds looming like ominous shadows, heralding the arrival of the impending tempest. The air grew heavy with anticipation, and distant thunder rumbled, sending shivers down his spine.

As the storm drew nearer, the atmosphere became charged with electricity, and flashes of lightning illuminated the sky with their jagged brilliance. The wind whispered through the trees, rustling their leaves in agitation. The scent of rain mingled with the earthy aroma of the countryside, filling the air with a sense of impending change.

Suddenly, the heavens opened, and rain poured down in torrents, drumming against the windows and rooftops with relentless force. Thunder boomed overhead, reverberating through the asylum walls and stirring the souls within.

As the storm raged outside, the painter seemed more agitated than usual. His hands trembled, not with the palsy of age or the acute withdrawal of absinthe, but with an inner turmoil that begged for release. The professor approached, placing a comforting hand on the painter's shoulder.

"Tell me, friend," the professor implored, "what troubles you so?"

The painter's eyes met his, a tempest of blue and green, and he whispered, "I am incomplete. My work, my soul, everything feels... unfinished."

The professor nodded, understanding the weight of unfulfilled dreams. "Perhaps," he suggested gently, "it is not completion we should seek, but the beauty of the process itself."

The painter pondered this, and for a moment, a serene smile graced his lips. "Yes, perhaps you are right," he conceded.

They stood together in silence, observing the chaos unleashed by the storm, yet amidst its fury, there existed a certain beauty that captivated them both. But as swiftly as the storm seemed to have formed out of thin air, it vanished just as quickly. The clouds dissipated, unveiling the night sky adorned with twinkling stars, while the crescent moon gleamed brightly overhead. The town below lay in silence, with only the crickets continuing their nocturnal symphony.

The painter stood, gazing at the night sky with a mixture of wonder and contemplation, though his mind perceived it differently from his eyes. Pausing briefly, he reached for a blank canvas from the stack beside him. Lost in his own thoughts, he ignored the professor next to him, hurriedly smearing cobalt blue onto the pristine surface as if racing against borrowed time.

The professor watched in fascination as the painter's brush strokes seemed to dance across the canvas, capturing the essence of the night sky in a way words could never do justice. Each stroke was deliberate yet imbued with a sense of urgency, as if the painter sought to encapsulate the fleeting beauty of the storm's aftermath.

As dawn broke, replacing the blue of the sky with hues of orange and pink, the professor felt a strange compulsion to ask the question that had lingered in his mind for so long.

"My friend," the professor began tentatively, "in all our time together, I've never asked your name. Would you tell me?"

The painter set down his brush, the corners of his mouth lifting in a bittersweet smile. "Vincent," he said simply. "My name is Vincent."

29

THE FLORIST

Nestled close to the shimmering coastline of Lake Michigan, in Chicago's most affluent neighborhood, the Gold Coast, stands a tiny flower shop that has been a sanctuary of stories for decades. Ms. Brenner, a spirited and dedicated woman, has been the heart and soul of this charming store since the 1970s. She took over the business from her father, who had inherited it from his own father, keeping the legacy alive.

The shop, named 'Flora' after Ms. Brenner's grandmother, was more than just a place to buy flowers. It was a repository of memories, a silent witness to countless moments of joy and sorrow. From the grand celebrations of births and birthdays to the tender moments of reconciliation marked by bouquets from repentant lovers, Flora was there. It provided elegant arrangements for anniversaries and offered solace through the delicate beauty of funeral wreaths. Through every chapter of life's journey, Flora stood as a testament to enduring love and remembrance, a constant in the ever-changing tapestry of time.

Each morning, Ms. Brenner, with her silver-streaked hair pulled into a neat bun, would carefully arrange fresh flowers outside the shop. The vibrant array of roses, lilies, and tulips seemed to beckon passersby, inviting them into a world where time slowed down and memories blossomed. She remembered the stories her father told her, of how her grandfather would spend hours perfecting bouquets while her grandmother hummed tunes from a bygone era. Even as cancer stole her strength, she maintained the shop with unwavering dedication, finding peace in the familiarity of her routine.

Ms. Brenner lived a modest life, content with the company of her flowers and the stories they silently witnessed. She had never married, dedicating her life to the shop and its memories, providing a little slice of heaven amid the bustling life around her. Flowers upon flowers stood in large silver vases on the wooden floors; eucalyptus, ferns, ivy, and other greenery towered all the way to the ceiling, making Flora look like a tropical island amid a concrete jungle. There was peace in the silence.

One brisk autumn morning, as Ms. Brenner arranged a particularly stunning bouquet of red roses, she greeted her regulars with a warm smile, her eyes twinkling with a kindness that made everyone feel at home. Sometimes, she would find herself pausing by the old wall in the back room, a warm look crossing her face as if she could hear whispers from the past. Neighbors often remarked on her peculiar habit, but she would just smile and change the subject. Little did they know that beneath her cheerful exterior, she was battling a silent adversary. Cancer had crept into her life, and despite her fierce will, it claimed her before her time.

With no close relatives, the future of Flora seemed uncertain. However, fate had other plans. Jack and Lisa, a young, inspiring couple with dreams of running their own business, took over the shop. They saw potential in Flora, envisioning a blend of old charm and new vitality. Jack and Lisa had dreamed of owning a business together since their college days. Jack, with his knack for business, and Lisa, with her creative flair, saw Flora as the perfect blend of their talents. Their decision to take over the shop was as much about preserving a piece of history as it was about forging their own path.

Jack and Lisa embarked on a journey of renovation, aiming to breathe fresh life into the beloved store. The renovation was a labor of love. They spent countless hours stripping old wallpaper, sanding down wooden beams, and carefully choosing new fixtures that maintained the shop's vintage charm. As they worked, they occasionally found small mementos of the past—an old ledger, a faded photograph—which hinted at the rich history hidden within Flora's walls.

One evening, as the couple sifted through a box of old receipts in the back room, Jack noticed something peculiar. "Lisa, look at this," he said, holding up a receipt dated from the 1950s. "It's from a funeral home."

Lisa glanced at it and shrugged. "So? It makes sense. People have always used flowers for funerals."

Jack nodded, but couldn't shake the feeling that there was more to the story. A few days later, while demolishing a particularly stubborn section of wall, his hammer hit something solid and unexpected.

"Lisa, come over here. You need to see this," Jack called out, his voice trembling with excitement and disbelief.

Lisa rushed over, her eyes widening as she took in the sight. Hidden in the wall, stacks of money lay silently, neatly organized, among boxes filled with cassette tapes, cataloged by years.

"Jesus, Jack. This has to be over a million dollars! What do we do with all this?"

Jack, ever the pragmatist, replied, "First, we need to listen to these tapes. We might find out if they're connected to the money. There has to be a reason they were hidden."

Beside the box, they found an old cassette player. Jack dusted it off before inserting the first tape labeled "Schwartz funeral October 7, 1951." The machine crackled to life, and they heard the distant, grainy voices of people paying their respects to the dead. One by one, each tape revealed snippets of conversations, confessions, and secrets shared in the presence of funeral wreaths and flowers, their origins shrouded in the sorrow and vulnerability of loss.

Lisa shivered as she listened. "These… these are people's private moments. But why were they recorded? And how?"

Jack frowned, deep in thought. "We need to listen to them to find out. It's certainly strange." As they continued to go through each tape, a particularly chilling pattern emerged, revealing something sinister. Beside the sobbing voices and loving goodbyes, each cassette contained chilling revelations of the cause of the deceased, making it almost a confession. *"Sorry Mary that you had to suffer. If I knew I would have used more poison, although you made me suffer for decades—I'm free now."* The ominous tones sent as hiver down their spines.

"I think they put a bug into the wreaths," Jack concluded.

"Do you think Ms. Brenner blackmailed these people?" Lisa asked in disbelief.

"And her father and grandfather before her. That'd explain the money and the old ledger. They must have used these recordings to leverage people if the deceased was a victim of a homicide," Jack said as he paused the cassette player.

Lisa's hand flew to her mouth. "Murder?"

Jack rewound the tape, listening to the haunting words again. He looked at the stacks of cash and then back at Lisa.

"We can't just ignore it. Should we call the police?" Lisa kept probing Jack.

Jack looked at her, determination hardening his features. "No."

They carefully put the bricks back into place, ensuring the hidden compartment was once again concealed. That evening, as they sat in their cozy apartment above the shop, Jack placed an order for a set of listening devices. Lisa watched him, a mixture of fear and resolve in her eyes. They were stepping into a legacy of shadows, a history entwined with secrets and deception. But with it came the promise of security and success.

In the quiet of the night, the shop below stood silent, its flowers a testament to the passage of time and the secrets hidden within its walls. Jack and Lisa, bound by their newfound knowledge, faced a future where they too would carry the weight of Flora's legacy, blending innocence with the shadows of the past.

30

COGITO, ERGO RECONSIDERO

The Reconsidered Mind

In the bustling heart of a modern metropolis stood a man named Marcus. A man of intellect and ambition, Marcus navigated the maze of city streets with a confident stride, his mind buzzing with the constant hum of contemporary life. Yet, beneath the facade of productivity and purpose, a profound existential question gnawed at his consciousness: What does it truly mean to exist in the 21st century?

Marcus was no stranger to philosophical pondering. Raised in a world inundated with information and technological marvels, he'd been exposed to a myriad of philosophical concepts from a young age. But it was René Descartes' famous dictum that'd always resonated with him: *"Cogito, ergo sum"*—"I think, therefore I am." It was a mantra that had guided him through many turbulent seas of uncertainty, providing a steadfast anchor in the storm of existence.

However, as Marcus delved deeper into the complexities of modern life, he began to question the adequacy of Descartes'

219

proclamation. The idea of existence seems to transcend simple thought in a time of rapid technological advancements and ever-expanding virtual worlds. In a world where artificial intelligence and virtual realities blurred the lines between the real and the simulated, could the act of thinking alone suffice as proof of existence?

Thus, Marcus found himself embarking on a philosophical journey of introspection and inquiry, seeking to unravel the intricacies of contemporary existence. He pondered the nature of consciousness in an age of artificial intelligence, the significance of human experience in a world saturated with digital simulations, and the elusive boundaries between reality and illusion.

As Marcus delved deeper into his philosophical musings, he came to a startling realization: perhaps Descartes' dictum needed to be revised for the modern era. *"Cogito, ergo reconsidero"* —"I think, therefore I should reconsider." It was a subtle yet profound shift in perspective, one that encapsulated the essence of contemporary existence.

For Marcus, the act of thinking was no longer merely a means of affirming his existence; it was a call to constant reconsideration and reevaluation. In a world where reality itself seemed to be in a constant state of flux, the ability to question and reassess one's understanding of existence became paramount.

And so, armed with his newfound mantra, Marcus embarked on a quest for truth and meaning in the tumultuous landscape of the modern era. He delved into the depths of virtual realities, challenging the boundaries of perception and consciousness. He engaged in spirited debates with artificial intelligence, probing the nature of sentience and self-awareness. And through it all, he remained steadfast in his commitment to the principle of constant reconsideration.

As Marcus gazed out at the sprawling cityscape before him, he felt a sense of awe and wondered at the boundless possibilities of the universe. And though the questions of existence would continue to perplex and elude him, he took comfort in the knowledge that the journey of thought and reconsideration would never cease.

In the end, Marcus emerged not with definitive answers but with a profound sense of purpose and clarity. For him, existence was no longer a static state to be taken for granted but a dynamic process of continual questioning and exploration. And in embracing the mantra of *"Cogito, ergo reconsidero,"* he found solace in the ever-unfolding mystery of existence itself. It wasn't the certainty of his existence that defined him, but the relentless pursuit of truth and understanding in an ever-changing world.

And as long as he continued to think, to question, and to reconsider, he knew that he would always 'be', in some form or another.

222

AFTERWORD

As I reflect on the journey that brought this collection to life, I'm filled with a sense of accomplishment and gratitude. This compilation represents more than just a year of dedicated effort; it encapsulates the very essence of our shared human experience. Each story, poem, and piece within these pages is a fragment of the mosaic of our emotions, capturing the diverse stages we traverse in life.

In crafting these works, we delved into the depths of introspection, embraced the lightness of humor, navigated the stormy seas of frustration, and stood firm in the face of righteous anger. These stories are not mere words on a page; they're reflections of the breadth of human experience, each one a mirror to our own lives.

Thank you for allowing these stories into your life and for being a part of this shared exploration of the human condition. Your presence as a reader brings these words to life, and for that, I am deeply grateful.

A.P. Harper